McKinley
The Witch Of Ivanov

Sharlene Frances
Writing From the Heart

PUBLICATION
CONSULTANTS
We Believe In The Power Of Authors

8370 Eleusis Drive, Anchorage, Alaska 99502-4630
books@publicationconsultants.com—www.publicationconsultants.com

ISBN Number: 978-1-63747-415-0
eBook ISBN Number:978-1-63747-416-7

Library of Congress Number: 2024945518

Manufactured in the United States of America

To my three darling sisters:
Lols, Megs and Sammy-Lamb.
and my amazing Mom.
Thank you for all the love, laughter and not to
forget, the drama!
What family is complete without it?

LIVE LIFE TO THE FULL

LOVE YOUR LIFE

LAUGH WITH YOUR WHOLE HEART

Table of Contents

Chapter 1 — The Test Subject..7

Chapter 2 — The Village Witch... 14

Chapter 3 — You Are Supposed To Be Scary......................... 24

Chapter 4 — The Witch Creator... 31

Chapter 5 — The Terror Of Ivanov 38

Chapter 6 — Trouble Personified 52

Chapter 7 — She Would Never!.. 61

Chapter 8 — A Witch? More Like A Demon From Hell.......... 71

Chapter 9 — Meanwhile, Back At The Ranch....................... 77

Chapter 10 — Whatever .... (Rolling Eyes) 81

Chapter 11 — Be Afraid, Be Very Afraid.............................. 89

Chapter 12 — Wolves And A Blizzard.
            This Is Russia After All..................................... 96

Chapter 13 — Letting The Cat Out Of The Bag.................. 102

Chapter 14 — Cookies and Goggles 107

Chapter 15 — Home... 112

Chapter 16 — Conclusion 116

Acknowledgments 118

Table of Contents

Chapter 1 – The Test Subject

Ivanov – Eastern Russia:

McKinley is stuck. She hasn't a clue about romance, and this online writing course is expecting her to write a love scene. With feeling . . . get under the characters' skin . . . use all your senses. I mean, really? As far as she is concerned, love and romance belong in fantasy fiction. Everything she writes sounds so annoyingly pathetic, and her attempt at 'steamy and unforgettable' would do well in a cheesy comedy. She stares thoughtfully out of the window. She needs help.

The prospect of help comes in the form of Sascha, who just happens to be walking by that very window. Mmm . . . she could do with a different perspective. He is a man after all and with his gorgeous looks and untamed Russian heart, he should have had plenty of experience with 'hot and steamy'. The thought of Sascha making wild, passionate love with some other woman makes her heart feel heavy and her stomach clench uncomfortably. Where on earth does that come from? Forcing the images from her mind, she opens the window and leans out to intercept her quarry as he is on his way to the garage.

"Hey, Sasch!"

Sascha freezes mid-step, then turns and regards her suspiciously. She is not going to catch him again. No matter how enticing and innocent she may seem, it is never the case. What hare-brained scheme is she cooking up now? More importantly, does he really want to get involved? She is hanging halfway out the window looking like the angel he knows she isn't, waving at him to come inside. This cannot be good.

"I just need your help for a few minutes. It won't take too long." She is far too charming.

Against his better judgment, Sascha makes his way to the house. Standing below the window, he looks up at her with his hands on his hips. No nonsense.

"What do you need?" Maybe there is no harm in asking. Yeah, sure.

She is looking far too pleased with herself. Her smile widens and her odd-colored eyes gleam with triumph.

"Please, my darling Sasch, tell me what you think of this love scene."

"Now?" He looks up at her with raised eyebrows. He really does not have the time to read some soppy love story.

"Why not? Come on in and sit at the table. I will read it to you."

Meeting him at the door, she leads her captive to the table. Sascha watches as she takes a chair in front of her laptop, and scans through the story. It must be her eyes that do it to him every time. One eye is rich blue, as bright as a summer sky; the other is as gray and as stormy as a winter sea. That hair of hers is no help either. Long and dark, a shimmering torrent of unruly curls, you would think that would be good enough, but noooo...... it also has to be streaked with white-blond. What crazy stuff was going on when she was put together, one can only guess.

As McKinley starts to read out the first few words she begins to laugh. This is so bad! Soon she is laughing so hard that she cannot get a word out edgeways.

"Hold on, I can't do this." She gasps leaping up, she pushes him into the chair.

"Okay, sit here. You can read it to yourself then tell me what you think."

Still smiling, she flops down and sprawls across the sofa. Sighing, she closes her eyes. Sascha stares across at her, then down at the screen.

"This is American."

"I know, is that a problem?"

"Mmm........." He is mumbling under his breath, and McKinley catches something involving 'hot-blooded and fire'

"Just read it, Sasch. Who cares about fiery hearts and all that other 'goodness knows what'?"

A doubtful smile touches his lips and he looks back at the screen. He starts slowly scrolling down, his eyebrows climbing higher with every second.

"Oh....... okay...." He is smiling now.

She opens one eye. "What?"

"Nothing.... huh!" Now he has a wide smile that he cannot control.

McKinley sits up. She *knew* it! The scene *is* reading like a wretched comedy.

"Now what?" she demands.

"Nothing," he assures her, but he continues to mumble a string of choice words under his breath. Mac can hear only some of what he says from where she is sitting, and none of it is very complimentary.

"Will you just tell me?" She is thinking that this was not such a good idea.

"Shhhh!" He flaps his hand at her. "Pipe down, Mac, I need to concentrate."

She hates to be shushed; he knows that it will irritate the dickens out of her. How good is this, to have her on the back foot for a change? Only problem is, he is absolutely going to pay for it, one way or another.

At last Sascha looks up and stares at her, his eyebrows raised and a huge grin on his face.

"Okay, spit it out, mister." And she braces herself for the worst.

"Well, firstly, guys don't kiss like that."

"Oh, really?" This is going to be more complicated than she thought. "What's the difference?"

"Your guy is a wuss – what's his name? Robbie? Bobbie?"

"Henry."

"Henry? Sheesh, that sucks." Sascha starts laughing and she frowns at him.

"Okay, Mac." He is starting to enjoy himself now. "First he must test the waters."

"Test the waters? What do you mean by that?"

"Well, 'Henry' does not want to get slapped, does he?" Sascha's silver-gray eyes are sparkling now. "If he just dives in like that – he will probably get slapped." He starts laughing. "Even in Russia," he adds.

Actually, that does make some sense. If a guy just came and slobbered all over her, she would certainly give him a good slap. She gets up from the couch and goes to stand next to Sascha.

"Okay – so test the waters – what do you mean? How does he do that?"

"You want me to show you?" To his credit, Sascha is managing to keep a straight face.

"Sure, why not? Pretend you are Jeffery, er – Henry – or whoever."

Chapter 1 — The Test Subject

"Okay." Sascha gets to his feet. Standing close to Mac, he slides his hands down her arms. He takes her by the hands and draws her closer.

McKinley closes her eyes and waits. She can feel the heat of his body close to hers. Nothing happens. Opening one eye, she sees him staring at her. He is smiling again.

"Now what?"

"You are too tense; you need to loosen up."

"What? Like have a drink?"

"Sure. It is only eight in the morning, but – you can do that if you want to......."

"Um, no." Mac shakes her head, her eyes shining with laughter.

Sascha is staring at her thoughtfully. This girl is stunning in every way. Nineteen years old now, her unusual beauty has only become more tantalizing as she has grown. He can hardly keep his hands off her at the best of times. He knows that she is big trouble with a capital 'T'.

"What?" McKinley is suddenly aware of the way he is watching her.

"How come you don't know about any of this stuff, Mac? What is wrong with the boys in the village?"

Mac looks at the man standing so close to her. He is perfect; he is her hero, her best friend. He can do no wrong. The boys in the village don't come anywhere near him. Besides that, they are all terrified of her.

"Enough questions, Sasch." She grins up at him. "Now go ahead and 'test the waters'. Kiss me like you don't want to get slapped."

She expects him to kiss her then; she expects to feel his mouth on hers. Instead, he lifts her hand and starts kissing her fingers, his eyes never leaving hers. Her stomach lurches and her heart hammers in her chest. What the heck? How can he make her feel this way just by kissing her fingers? Oh no! If he kisses her on the mouth now, she is likely to burst into flames and explode on the spot.

"Um, Sasch." Swallowing hard, Mac tries to pull her hand from his. She tries to back away.

"Is there a problem, little witch?" His hand tightens around hers, pulling her closer instead. It is what she sees behind his smiling eyes that makes her knees turn to water; that makes her insides clench; that makes her feel extremely hot and bothered.

"Um, Sasch." He is looking at her now with a raised eyebrow, his mouth twitching on the edge of a very wide smile. "I don't think the boss will appreciate it if his house burns down."

"What?"

"I am sure of it," she says with conviction. "If you were to kiss me now, I would simply combust and everything would go up in............"

Mac instantly forgets what she was about to say as he pulls her into his arms and his lips find hers. Every single thought she has ever possessed is burned away with a melting need to...to what? Her mind is mush; she has no clue how to handle the magnitude of emotion that is swamping her heart and engulfing her mind.

Sascha's intention of giving Mac just a quick demonstration turns into something deeper and a lot more serious as soon as he tastes her. He cannot help pulling her closer, feeling her melt against him, her soft, warm lips moving on his, asking him to give her more. Her hands slide up over his chest and she wraps her arms around his neck, curling her fingers into his hair. What is he doing? The boss is going to kill him. Why does he never heed his wise inner voice where this woman is concerned? Mac is trouble, but he is already addicted to her; addicted to her laugh, addicted to her madness, addicted to all that McKinley does, all that she is. Now he has gone and made it much worse. Within seconds he has become addicted also to her lips, to her body pressed against his; addicted to her scent . . . warm, sweet, and flowery.

With an effort, Sascha tears his mouth from hers. She stares up at him, her eyes glowing, soft, and bottomless. He backs away from her, battling to breathe. Dropping his hands to his sides, he turns and strides out of the room and straight out of the house.

Phew! Mac is on fire. Her mind is buzzing; she feels both frustrated and energized. The feel of Sascha's body, so hot and strong, the touch of his lips, have set her on fire, a fire that has now been awakened and will never be entirely quenched. The feel of his arms around her, pulling her closer. . . Sheesh, she can hardly breathe. Her whole body is urging her to go after him, to pull him back into her arms, to kiss him again, to kiss him for longer.

She turns and faces the laptop. Wow! If she tries to put that into words, her laptop will just crash and burn. Whether it is written in Russian or any other language in the world, the effects will certainly be the same. A big bang and a lot of fire and smoke.

Chapter 2 – The Village Witch

Another village in Eastern Russia – four years ago

With the ending of the Soviet Union, many of the small settlements and villages in Russia lost their income and were soon forgotten and desolate. Most people left to find a better life in the cities and larger towns. For the few that remained, life was hard and they found it better to work together. The huntsmen of this village deep in Eastern Russia contributed by fishing for salmon, herring and whatever else they could find in the freezing sea and fast-flowing rivers. They hunted for meat in the surrounding wilderness. There were plenty of Siberian grouse, reindeer, and the occasional Snow Sheep that came into the area. There were also many dangers; the polar bear was a frequent visitor to these shores as was the giant brown bear. The Siberian tiger was a very rare and beautiful sight, but nonetheless, no hunter wanted to come across one of those. The weather was the worst enemy of all. Moving in fast, the winter storms were ruthless to any caught without shelter.

The survival skills of a huntsman had to be extensive to survive this unforgiving land they called home.

McKinley grew up in this small village on the wild, forgotten coastline of Eastern Russia. Her mother had wanted to give her a good Russian name, Sima, which means 'a treasure', but that name had gone out the window pretty fast. Mac's dad, Nicholai Orlov, was fanatical about the mountains around the world. He was one of the town's most experienced hunters; he was also a guide, a climber, and an adventurer. His work took him away from home for weeks, sometimes months, at a time. The kids in the family were all named after famous mountains: Logan, Everest, Kenya, Elbert, and Elbrus. The suggestion of McKinley gave rise to a bit of a debate, but her dad had climbed that mountain before the name was changed to Denali, and he had decided on McKinley. Her mother went along with whatever he wanted; she would do anything and everything for her wonderful, brave, and crazy man.

Six years ago, when the youngest of the Orlov tribe was just a few months old, Nicholai had left on yet another expedition. He had been hired as a guide to a party of explorers who were keen to discover the hidden secrets of the Golden Mountains of Altai – a paradise for one such as Nicholai Orlov, who considered that entire range to be the Garden of Eden. He was supposed to be away for four months, but the months turned into a year, and he never returned. Mac will never forget the day the news eventually came that her Pops would not be coming home. There had been a freak storm followed by an avalanche that had wiped out the entire party. There were no survivors. Ten-year-old Mac felt as though her heart had been torn out . . . never again to hear his easy laugh, or his mad jokes. . . The Orlov family was shredded with grief. McKinley's mother was devastated, and her children were the only reason that she did not follow her darling Nicholai into the next life. The year that followed was the hardest of all as the family came to full understanding that their anchor would never again be there to calm the stormy waters of life, that they were only existing, with huge chunks of their hearts missing forever. The younger children grew up with the consequences, not quite understanding the constant darkness that lay behind every smile.

McKinley had her father's resilience, his keen and crazy mind, his brave and generous heart. Her strength was a beacon for her family in the blackest of times, and her antics and schemes became a distraction and a source of happy disruption. Slowly the family knitted back together, finding strength and healing within a circle of warmth and love.

In the village, McKinley was known as *Koldun'ya* –Russian for witch or sorceress. She was a freak; even she would admit it. Both parents and her five siblings had straight hair and eyes that are almost black, as had the rest of the people in her part of the world. Mac's dark hair was not only a wild mess of curls but was also liberally streaked with white-blond. Not quite like Cruella De Vil, but close enough that she had heard most of the jokes in that vein. Her eyes were not only blue, unusual in itself, but they were also two different colors of blue. Summer and winter, was how her Pops used to describe them. Everyone, including herself, wondered where on earth the strange coloring came from.

It was because of her unusual looks that Dimitri Komarov came to hear of her and took immediate interest. She would make the perfect witch, and the people in his village, as well as those far and wide, would certainly show him a great deal of respect should he have someone such as her in his household.

The people who still lived in those forgotten villages, in the middle of an Arctic wasteland, were a superstitious lot. They were strong believers in supernatural signs and omens. And why not?

The land they lived in was unforgiving, the weather was extreme and the dangers were many. It was always good to have a heads-up if something bad was going to happen, no matter what the source.

Dimitri Komarov. What a blockhead. It was during the summer, and Mac had just turned sixteen, when Komarov came to check her out. He had traveled from a large town a couple hundred miles away from her village. Driving one of those all-terrain vehicles that the hunters normally used, he came roaring up the track that they all proudly called a road and halted dramatically in front of the house. Mac's mother went to the gate, along with an assortment of kids, curious to know what such a rich man was doing at their door. Two men exited from the growling beast. They were smartly dressed, modern, looking like city people. Mac's family were immediately impressed. A young man, tall, lean, and athletic, stood aside to allow the other, massive with florid skin, a large red nose, and blubbery lips, to precede him. This impressed the family even more. Imagine how much this man must eat to gain such massive proportion: he must be loaded! They welcomed him into the house like a king.

Rudely ignoring the family's greeting and invitation, the big red-faced man turned to the young man at his side. "Are you sure you have the right family?" he huffed irritably. "I see no one remotely unusual here."

"I am sure. I have seen her myself."

Sascha would not forget in a hurry, the day that he first laid eyes on the girl. He had just completed some business in this part of the world and was on his way home when he was almost run right off the road by a girl flying past him in a golf cart. Her bizarre hair was streaming out around her, her astonishing eyes sparkling brightly with sheer devilry. He had no idea that those little carts could move so fast, never mind over a road that was only suited for a 4x4 truck. She laughed when she saw his incredulous expression, then tooted the little horn and waved. He could swear that she winked at him. Before he knew what was happening, she veered off the track and shot off, bouncing into an open field, she careened over a grassy hill and disappeared.

He had enquired in the nearby village.

"Oh . . ." People nodded with exasperated sighs. "That can only be *Koldun'ya*. What has she done now?"

Mac was sitting up in a tree, reading a book. Another mark in the 'weird column' for her, because few people in the village read books and their library was sadly understocked. She had read every book at least twice. Of course, girls sitting in trees were also considered weird.

"McKinley! Come down, there is a man to see you." Her mam was using her proper name; this had to be serious.

"A man? What do you mean? What kind of man? Is it the police again? I swear I put her golf cart back where I found it, there was hardly a scratch or a dent on it."

Her mother looked up at Mac. She didn't even bother asking. The story would be complicated, and one that she did not need to know about, thank you very much! .... Mind you, Mrs. Petrovna, the village baker, had seemed inexplicably grumpy lately, eyeing her with lashings of disapproval – and the baker was the only person for many miles who owned such an ostentatious thing as a golf cart. Mac's mother decided that it was best not to dwell on it too much.

"No, nothing like that." Mac's mam shrugged. "Come with me, I will help you clean up."

Mac leaped agilely from the top branch, landing in a perfect superhero pose right in front of her mother – crouched with a hand on the ground, an arm extended out behind her. Looking up at her mam, she started laughing.

"Oh dear. Poor Mr. Komarov, he really does not know what he is in for." Her mother sighed, taking Mac's hand.

"I have to do what?" Mac stared at her mother, not sure she had heard her correctly.

"Mr. Komarov has made a very generous offer for you and he would like to meet you."

Mac's eyebrows shot up and for the first time in her life, she was rendered speechless. And then she laughed.

"You are joking, right? The old guy?"

"Well . . ." Her mam smiled. "He is a bit old, but he is not *ancient*."

"Oh no, mam, he is closer to ancient." Mac lowered her voice. "Besides, what is with the red face and heavy breathing? Can he even...........you know."

"McKinley!" Her mother was appropriately appalled.

"It looks like he might die of a heart attack before he even gets started." As usual, the look on her mother's face only encouraged Mac more.

"How on earth do you know about such things, young lady?" Her mother was shocked. It seemed she had been shocked from the day her daughter was born. She should be used to it by now.

"I read." Mac laughed. "You would be surprised at the kind of books there are in that library of ours."

Mac's younger siblings all filed into the room: 'the Foothills', as she laughingly called them. They were going to miss their larger-than-life older sis; she was completely nuts, she made them laugh, and she kept life interesting. Things would be very dull without her around.

"Mam." Mac became serious. "How come you are letting me go to such a man?"

Mac's mother worked at brushing the leaves out of her wayward daughter's hair, trying to tame it into submission. This girl was far too wild to go to anyone like Mr. Komarov, but she did not have much choice. To refuse a rich and powerful man like Dimitri Komarov would be asking for trouble. He could make life extremely difficult, not only for Mac and her family, but for the whole village. So, the next best thing would be to make him pay through that bulbous nose of his for her heartbreak.

"Oh, my *Myshka*, I just want to do what is best for you." Her mother drew her into her arms and hugged her tightly. "You could do a lot worse than a large, wealthy, red-faced, ancient man."

No matter how hard Mac tried, she could not think of too many examples.

"What, mam, like if he lived in a mud hut with pigs and ate raw onions?"

"Or. . . " chimed in one of her sisters helpfully, ". . . if he is a tiny, thin, weakling of a man, and he lives with his very loud and over-bearing mother who expects you to be her personal servant."

"Mmm, yes, that would be bad....... I would hate to be anyone's personal servant....."

"Or......." The two boys laughed. "Blimey, what if he makes you sew and cook? That would be a cursed nightmare!"

"Boys!" Their mother glared at them. "Language! Where did you hear those words?"

Need she even ask? The boys started giggling, although they were adamantly shaking their heads. They looked straight at their older sister, their dark eyes shining with glee.

Her mam stepped back, keeping a hold of her daughter's hands.

"McKinley, my *Myshka*, we will miss you terribly. You are strong and brave just like your Pops; I know that you will be just fine." Her tone was very serious. "You are more powerful than you think; do not let others see it too easily."

Her mother often came out with odd little bits of ominous-sounding information and Mac had learned to accept them at face value; they ended up making sense in retrospect. Which is then a bit late, of course.

Mac was made to stand in the middle of the lounge while Dimitri Komarov walked around her, nodding and muttering to himself.

"You may not wear these jeans, they are detestable. The t-shirt must go. You dress like a hooligan." He huffed.

"Well! I guess I can always walk around in my underwear, would that suit you?" Mac asked. She kept her tone light but her eyes were starting to blaze. She did not like this man.

Komarov spluttered to a halt in front of her, his face bright red. She hoped that he didn't explode; that would be gross. He did not bother addressing her, but turned instead to her mother who was trying to send messages to her daughter through meaningful looks.

"She will do, although she will need to work on her attitude."

"She is a free spirit, not easy to contain." This was her mother's way of warning him that she was unlike other girls.

The large man turned to his young assistant. "Sascha, see to the details. I will wait in the car."

Mac's mother was not an ignorant peasant; she was educated and sharp. Much haggling ensued, with poor Sascha having to go outside several times to confer with his boss.

Buying people was not unheard of, especially if you were buying a wife. In remote areas where it was difficult to find suitable spouses, it was quite common. To find a husband as well off and important as Dimitri Komarov for her daughter was very lucky indeed, but that was no reason to let the guy railroad her into a deal she was not happy with.

Mac's family were quiet with their goodbyes. It was not certain that they would see their wacky *Myshka* any time soon - if ever. Life was going to be very different without her around. There would certainly be fewer irate neighbors knocking at their door demanding to speak to *Koldun'ya*. Mac hugged each of her 'Foothills' in turn. She kept up the jokes and laughter, making sure to keep her eyes from showing her sorrow and despair at leaving her home, especially when her mother held her tight. Mac's mother was not fooled for a minute, but she in turn put on her brave face. There would be plenty of time later to let her heartbreak flow.

Komarov hurried Mac into the vehicle, keen to be on his way. He had no intention of marrying this strange person; he had other plans for her. As far as he was concerned, he had paid the money, so he could now do what he liked with her. Well, that was supposed to be the plan.

Mac hung out of the window, waving her arms wildly until the vehicle rounded a corner and her family disappeared from sight. She sat back and looked at the two men sitting quietly in the front. Far too quiet, far too peaceful. The challenge was far too great, far too tempting.

"So, Mr. Dimitri." Mac purposely confused his names; it was bound to irritate the heck out of him. "How far away is your house?" Mac leaned forward from the back seat and rested her arms along the back of Komarov's seat. Invading his space.

"We get there, when we get there." He shifted forward irritably. "You will address me as Mr. Komarov." This girl did not have one iota of an idea about manners, and no respect whatsoever.

Mac smiled, her sparkling eyes meeting the silver-gray eyes of Sascha in the rearview mirror. He was certainly not from her part of the country; must be from one of the big cities. His expression was both incredulous and full of shocked amusement. A reaction that Mac was very used to.

"Soooooo…….." Mac paused for effect; she had these guys at her mercy for long hours to come. "………. Are we there yet?"

The two men in the front exploded.

Komarov huffed, puffed, and exhaled loudly with exasperation, followed by a string of muttered curses.

Sascha had a coughing fit. He tried his hardest to keep a straight face, keeping his eyes on the road, not daring to meet those bright, wicked eyes in his rearview mirror. Mac leaned back, spreading her arms out along the back seat, smiling to herself. This guy, Dimitri Komarov, was easy to wind up; it would be child's play to distract him and get him off track. That was handy to know.

Chapter 3 – You Are Supposed To Be Scary

The trip took hours and nobody was ever more relieved to see the lights of Ivanov than Dimitri Komarov and Sascha. McKinley had kept up a running commentary the entire way, starting with reviews of all the books in the village library. She made a lot of them up, making the stories totally absurd – just to check if the two men were listening. She was rewarded with a lot of huffing and sighing from the front and again, the silver eyes gleaming at her in the rearview mirror. Getting bored with the books, she went on to review all the village people, then the kids and all the assorted pets and relatives. She was a never-ending treasure trove of trivia, excitedly gifting her companions with nuggets of information about things that nobody in the world could possibly give a toss about.

It did not take her long to discover the electric window buttons in the doors. Ooohh . . . this would be an endless source of fun. She spent a while opening and closing the windows, first on the left, then on the right, then both together – that took quite a bit of stretching, to press both buttons at the same time. Her fun was abruptly and rudely brought to a halt when Sascha locked her windows from the front. Their eyes met in the mirror, both pairs shining with amusement. Mac was delighted at how annoyed Komarov could get, his muttering becoming more and more colorful and graphic with every turn of the wheels.

As they got closer to the town, Mac finally became quiet. Never in her entire life had she seen so many lights all in one place. It seemed to her to be an ocean filled with fireflies. Looking at her in the mirror, Sascha watched as she stared out of the dark window, her eyes never leaving the vista before her, a smile of delight lighting her face. Even in the darkness of the car, he could see her wonder. Smiling to himself, he shook his head. If all it took were a few lights to shut her up, he would have come up with a plan a lot sooner.

Komarov was of course the mayor of Ivanov, as well as the most prominent businessman. He owned most of the commercial sector, and more than half of the residential properties belonged to him. He was a hard and impatient man, without a scrap of conscience or compassion for his fellow citizens. He would stoop to any level to add to his already sizeable wealth. As they drove up to his mansion just outside the town, Mac was suitably impressed.

"That house is huge! How many in your family, Mr. Dimitri?"

Komarov did not bother to acknowledge this irritating scrap of a girl. He turned to Sascha.

"Drop me at the front door. Take the girl with you, Anya will know what to do with her." He eyed Mac, who was grinning at him from the back seat. "I hope," he muttered. He could not get out of the vehicle fast enough.

No sooner had Komarov vacated the front seat, than Mac climbed over from the back and took his place.

"Come on, Sasch." She smiled at the startled young man at the wheel. "Now that we have ditched Mister Grumpy, you can show me the town."

"I don't think so, Madam McKinley." He laughed. "Anya is waiting for us with supper, are you not hungry?"

"Ravenous! Lead the way."

When Anya the housekeeper had been told that the boss was going to bring a witch back from a village farther up the coast, she hadn't known exactly what to think or what to expect. She had prepared a room, made it comfortable, even added a vase of flowers. She had made a wonderful rich soup and baked her dense and satisfying dark bread – and then she started second guessing herself. What on earth do witches eat? Do they even sleep at night? If they do sleep, do they sleep on a normal bed, or is it a special bed made of nails? Or the bones of their victims? Or maybe a coffin . . . . oh no, she mentally shook her head: that would be vampires. Should she supply a broom, or would the witch have her own? What about a cauldron? Oh well. . . Anya sighed. She had best wait for the person to arrive then ask about all these things.

Komarov had purposely leaked the news that a witch was coming to town. The whole community was abuzz with rumors and stories, most of them gruesome and evil. Anya could not help being just a little apprehensive. The longer she waited, the more horrific the stories in her head became. When she eventually heard the front door open, she almost jumped out of her skin and had to stop herself from diving under the kitchen table. Peeking around the door, she saw that it was just the boss. He was muttering and ranting to himself, looking distinctly out of sorts. Coming forward to take his hat and coat, she greeted him, and asked politely if he would like to eat downstairs and if the witch was here, would she also be joining him?

He stood stock-still, staring at her. The very idea of spending another minute in the company of that wretched girl filled him with horror. Anya misunderstood the look on his face and wrung her hands in panic, her thoughts racing. *Oh dear, is she that bad? What have we done bringing such evil into our house?*

26

"You can bring my supper up to me, Anya. I will be in my office. Under no circumstances does that girl come near my door."

Anya watched white-faced, her heart in her mouth, as her boss lumbered up the stairs. A commotion at the back kitchen door had her dithering around in the hallway, not sure whether to rush out of the front door while the going was good, or to return to the kitchen.

"Anya!" Sascha was calling her; hopefully he was okay and hadn't been turned into a frog. He sounded fine. But then, she had no clue what a Sascha-frog might sound like. Putting her shoulders back, she took a deep calming breath. She could do this! With authority, she entered her kitchen with a confidence she absolutely did not feel . . . and came face to face with mischief personified.

"Anya." Sascha grinned at her confused face. "I would like you to meet our most wicked and evil witch in the whole of Russia, if not the entire world – McKinley!"

"Mac . . ." He turned to the smiling girl at his side. "This is Anya, she takes care of all of us."

Before Anya could take a breath, the strange girl walked toward her and warmly took the housekeeper by the hand.

"*Tetya* Anya, I am so pleased to meet you." The girl kissed her respectfully on the cheeks, her odd-colored eyes showing warmth and her beautiful face glowing with pleasure.

Although the very last person Mac would have wanted to irritate was the person who cooked the food, that thought was farthest from her mind. She felt a genuine liking for this plump, older woman with the rosy cheeks and graying hair. Anya felt like home.

"My dear girl!" Anya was at a loss for words. Before her stood a young woman whose eyes shone like gemstones – sapphire, and diamond – fringed with the longest, thickest dark eyelashes. Despite her beauty, this girl had the naughtiest face that Anya had ever set eyes on. She understood now why her boss had reacted the way he did at the suggestion of dining with this imp. Laughter crept into the older woman's chocolate-brown eyes and her whole face crinkled with humor.

"Oh dear, Sasch, was the drive *very* long?"

"It took an eternity." Sascha laughed.

Mac woke up early, to the sound of a rooster crowing his head off just outside her window. For a few minutes, she was completely at a loss as to where she was. The bed she had slept in was the biggest bed she had ever laid eyes on and the mattress was quite bouncy; she knew that because of course she had tested it. With her head almost touching the ceiling at each jump on the mattress, Mac was more than satisfied with the bounciness of her new bed. Her room was spacious, with a large window at one end and a fireplace at the other. There was a wardrobe to keep her clothes in, for whenever she acquired more clothes – Anya had been dismayed to find that she had only a very small bag with her, filled mostly with books. Best of all, she had her very own bathroom. How cool was that?

There was a light tap on the door, and Anya came into the room.

"Oh good, you are awake." Anya bustled over to the window and opened the drapes. Soft, golden sunlight streamed into the room. "Come down to the kitchen for breakfast as soon as you are ready. I suspect you have a very busy day ahead."

A meeting had been called in the boss's office. Komarov sat behind his over-sized desk, tapping his pen impatiently on his desk pad, regarding the three people standing on the other side. His eyes shifted to the smallest one in the middle. She was smiling again. She should stop smiling and start acting like the witch that he had paid money for. He frowned at her and her smile widened.

"McKinley." Komarov would soon get her to stop smiling.

Mac was surprised that Komarov even knew her name; she had imagined that he thought she was called 'That Girl'.

"The reason you are here is simple. You are to be the Village Witch. Do you have any questions?"

Her answer was written all over Mac's face. Sascha and Anya mentally braced themselves, staring down at their shoes.

"Oh, yes, I do actually, thank you for asking." Mac's expression was serious and sincere, respectful even. The other two did not dare to look up, not even for a second.

"My broom . . . I left it with the mechanic in my old village. It was misfiring. Would I be able to get another one from your own village broom mechanic?" There was not a twitch of a smile on Mac's face. She shrugged and continued, taking care to hold her gaze steady on the popping eyes and the red, disbelieving face in front of her. "If you can spare the money, a new one would be better. You never know the problems that pre-owned brooms might have. Sometimes it is worth the extra money to buy them new, then they come with insurance and a service plan included – as well as the warranty."

Komarov slowly rose to his feet. He glared at the girl, his black eyes shining hard as stone, his face bright red. He was so angry that the wispy hair on his head was starting to stand up on end.

"McKinley," he grated out. "From now on you will do as I say to the letter, or I will make sure that your family suffer for your insufferable behavior." He leaned forward, placing his palms on the desk top.

"Rule number one: You will play your part, and that means no smiling! Rule number two: You may not joke around; you are to be nasty and evil. If I catch you being nice to anyone, or if I see even a twitch of a smile, then you will be sorry." He glared at the girl before him. The infuriating thing was, even with her face perfectly composed and her eyes serious, there was still that gleam of devilry, still the feeling that she was about to say or do something ludicrous at any moment.

"Sascha, I want you to take the girl to see Madame Tarasova. I have spoken to her and she knows what to do."

The young man jumped to attention, not sure that he had heard correctly. That did not sound like a good idea at all; he had absolutely no control of McKinley whatsoever.

"Would it not be better for Anya to take her? Or perhaps Madame Tarasova can come here?"

"No, it must be you. Make sure you are armed; I need everyone thinking the worst."

"You mean you want people to think that she is so dangerous, that I need to have weapons for protection?"

This time it was Mac and Anya who were staring fixedly down at their shoes. There were strange snorts coming from Mac. Komarov scowled at each of them in turn then shook his head.

"You are all useless! Get out of my sight." The three turned to file out of his office. "And you had better get this right. I do not want to hear anything good about our witch!" The boss had the final word, of course.

Chapter 4 – The Witch Creator

"Oh, please can I drive, Sasch?" Mac was bouncing alongside Sascha like an excited puppy. They were going to get to ride in a sleek black luxury car. One that glided over the back roads like it was hovering above the ground.

"No, Mac, you certainly may not drive. You have to sit in the back anyway."

"But that doesn't seem right. You cannot have a dangerous witch sitting behind you, she could put a spell on you and you wouldn't even know it."

"Oh yeah?" Sasch turned to look at her, his silver eyes full of laughter. "Where is your wand?"

"My wand?" Mac stared at him with narrowed eyes. Sascha could almost see the wheels in her head turning at full speed. Then she threw her shoulders back and looked down her nose at him, hard as that was to do when the person being looked down at is much taller.

"The batteries are flat." Mac spoke with absolute conviction, her face completely serious. She shrugged a shoulder. "I was going to ask Mr. Dimitri if I could replace them, but you saw how he be-

31

haved when I asked him for a new broom. He completely over-re-acted and was utterly unreasonable."

Sascha sighed. "Just get in the car, *Koldun'ya*. We are already late."

Madame Tarasova was not in a good mood. She had had her two assistants, Olga and Daria, come in earlier than usual and now she was whipping them both up into a frenzy of cleaning and sorting. Madame Tarasova had told the ladies that Dimitri Komarov was sending over a person for fittings, but she had not told them who that person was. It would not do to have her help running from the shop in terror just yet.

"Olga! I want all the black bolts we have, the purple and the dark red. Daria! Where are the measuring tape and the special scissors? I need everything on the table, now."

The last thing she wanted was for her business to be cursed because of some silly slip-up.

A vehicle drew up at the back of the shop. As Madame went to open the door, the two assistants looked out of the window.

"Ohhhhhh, wonderful! It is our gorgeous Sascha. That man is just delicious." Daria was almost drooling.

"He is coming into the shop! How lucky for us," Olga exclaimed, and the two women jostled one another to be the first to welcome him in and perhaps take his coat. They stopped short when they saw that he was not alone. At his side was a stunning young woman, a stranger to the village. Perhaps she was his sister . . . There was no way anyone could hope to compete with such a person.

"Oh, oh," Madame muttered under her breath. "And he has brought the witch."

"That is the witch?" whispered Olga incredulously. "No way!"

"She looks more like some kind of fairy princess," Daria breathed. "Wow!"

"Now girls, let us be our most professional!" Madame reminded them sternly.

The two shop assistants were surprised when their normally stuck-up boss rushed forward, gushing greetings and delivering a most elaborate, non-professional welcome.

The three women could not believe that this girl came anywhere close to being a witch, and they welcomed her enthusiastically and with much relief. Mac was taken aback by the sudden rush of people. In the small shop, it seemed like a flood of hand-shaking and cheek-kissing. She found herself standing closer to Sascha, threading her arm through his. These women must be on something, of that she was sure.

"Um, Madame . . ." Sascha saw that the indomitable McKinley was feeling overwhelmed. She must be human after all. Smiling, he turned to the dressmaker. "I would think only measurements are necessary now. If you have clothes that are ready-made, we will take those with us."

"Oh no, Mr. Sascha. Miss McKinley has to stay here for most of the day, we have a lot of work to get through. Mr. Komarov was very clear, and he expects only the best."

There were not only the sinister witch outfits that needed making up, but also hair and makeup to be done. Komarov did not do things in half measures and Madame Tarasova had had detailed instructions as to what the man wanted.

Madame was not joking. For many long hours, Mac was pulled, prodded, poked, and pricked until she had three witchy outfits complete with a hooded cape that kept her face in mysterious shadow.

"A cape?" She laughed, both horrified and amused. "You must be joking! Capes are for superheroes with insecurity issues. I refuse."

She had insisted on testing the outfits out. How could she climb up trees and onto roofs if her skirts were so narrow? How could she leap over fences and walls without decent tread on her long black boots?

Her hair was washed and brushed out, causing a lot of ooohs and aaaahs. The long shiny locks of black and white curls were beautiful, and the ladies took their time tending to them. Madame styled the hair, trimming and cutting, feathering, and layering. Mister Komarov had been adamant that curls were for cute little girls, not evil witches, but no matter what Madame did, she could not tame the curls - to make them sinister and straight. She shortened Mac's hair in the front to form black and white spikes that skimmed her finely-shaped dark brows, leaving the rest to fall in long, glossy curls. Not at all the plan, but Madame was fast learning that plans did not count one bit where this girl was concerned.

"I am going to show you how to do your makeup now, Miss McKinley. Please pay attention, it is important for all of our sakes that you get this right."

Mac was appalled at the amount of time and precision the whole application required. She could not see herself having the patience to do this every morning. But the end result was spectacular. She was transformed from McKinley to *Koldun'ya*. In the place of the fun-loving crazy young girl, stood a woman who was stunningly fierce and intimidating. Mac's own reflection just about scared her to death when she was shown the mirror. Pale-faced, with dark, gleaming eyes, she had become a creature of darkness and mystery. The very same scary creation who was then waved off by her three minions with much affection and laughter.

Sascha could not stop staring at Mac. The change in her appearance was astounding. She sat in the back seat, her face in shadow, but then she leaned forward.

"Sasch, I am starving! Those three slave drivers in there forgot that a witch has to eat."

He pulled over to the corner shop, and returned a few minutes later with a large bag of mini cookies and some soft drinks.

As he got in, Mac climbed out of the back of the car and joined him in front. It was late afternoon; the sun had started its downward journey toward the horizon. Racing clouds, thick and black, crowded out what was left of the blue sky and soon enough they blocked out the sun.

"If we eat these in this car, the boss will skin us alive and hang us out to dry." Sascha tucked the cookies away. "But have something to drink now, and it won't take long to get home."

The evilest witch in all of Russia gratefully took the small juice box. Expertly piercing the little straw into the hole, she handed it to Sascha then sorted out her own.

"Just how are you going to get people to fear you, Mac?" Sascha laughed. "Even if you look the part, people just cannot help but like you."

"Oh, don't worry about me, Sasch, I know how to scare the dickens out of people. They won't know what hit them." She grinned wickedly.

By the time they arrived home, the rain was already beginning to fall in large fat drops, and the ominous growling thunder was a continuous rumble. Sascha dropped Mac off at the kitchen door, then drove around to park the car in the extensive ten-vehicle garage. As Mac opened the door, a strong gust of wind wrenched it out of her hand causing it to slam against the wall. A bolt of lightning flashed, along with an almighty crash of thunder. At that same moment all the lights went out and she was silhouetted in the doorway, the storm raging wildly behind her. A shriek of terror exploded from the gloom of the large kitchen followed by a lot of banging, then Mac was pelted with yesterday's buns, tomatoes, and a few onions along with a barrage of extremely colorful language.

"Anya!" Mac shouted out, diving for cover. "It is only me – Mac."

"Oh, my goodness, Mac! I nearly shot you!" The relieved voice came from under the massive kitchen table.

"You have a gun?"

Anya was still not entirely convinced that it was Mac at the door. The person she had seen in that flash of lightning was not

Mac; it was a mythical creature with eyes that glowed from the depths of a hooded cloak, that flapped out around her like hideous bat wings.

"Um, yes. I have a very big gun, and I am not afraid to use it."

"Anya, put your water cannon away and stand down! We are coming in." Sascha's laughing voice came from behind Mac.

Getting the all-clear from the dangerously-armed housekeeper who had now emerged from under the table, Mac and Sascha were able to advance. Anya sheepishly tucked her brightly-colored plastic water pistol back under her apron. Mac caught Sascha staring accusingly at her, his eyebrows raised.

"What?" She laughed. "You think I did that on purpose?"

"I am not sure, *Koldun'ya* McKinley. It seemed a little too well-orchestrated."

"Well, Mr. Sascha, I guess you will never know, will you?" Mac's face was the picture of innocence. "Now you will spend long, sleepless nights wondering, 'did she, or didn't she?'"

It was a common occurrence for the lights to fail, especially during a storm, and candles and gas lamps were always on hand. Soon the kitchen and the rest of the house were flooded with the cozy glow of candles and filled with the warmth of fires.

The boss was upstairs, busy in his office. Anya told Sascha and Mac that he did not want to be disturbed; he would let them know when he was ready for their report. Taking advantage, the two went to change out of their drenched clothes and joined Anya in the toasty kitchen, warm and dry, for mugs of hot tea. Sascha produced the bag of cookies and the three were soon happily munching on those and sipping the tea.

"Do you know . . ." Mac leaned forward and looked at the other two closely, as if about to impart a very dark secret. They too leaned forward expectantly.

"I can fit sixteen of these in my mouth at one time."

"What?" exclaimed Anya. "Impossible."

36

"I bet that I can fit more," Sascha challenged.

"Never, Sasch. There is no way you can beat me, I am reigning champion."

"Prove it."

Their faces lit up with glee, all three started stuffing as many mini cookies as they could into their mouths. In no time they were looking like a trio of hamsters, with their cheeks stuffed to capacity, holding up fingers to signal to the others how many they had.

It was at that moment that Dimitri Komarov entered the kitchen. The intercom to the kitchen was not working because there was no power, so he had come in person to summon Sascha and Mac to his office. He certainly did not expect to encounter three people around the kitchen table, looking up at him with surprised, watering eyes, their cheeks puffed out like balloons and their faces as red as beets.

"Sascha, I need to speak to you in my office." He gestured vaguely. "And bring the girl." He backed slowly out, closing the door quietly behind him.

Chapter 5 – The Terror Of Ivanov

Over the next few weeks, Mac settled into Dimitri Komarov's household, it soon became clear that she was not at all what he had had in mind. Her idea of evil and nasty were not at all the same as his. People in the area became targets all right, but not in the way that was expected.

Mailman Igor was the first to suffer the wrath of *Koldun'ya*.

"How come Mailman Igor doesn't have any transport?" Mac asked Anya one day, watching the man walking away with his bag of mail weighing heavily on his shoulders.

"He does have a bicycle, but it is so old that he cannot use it. Mr. Komarov refuses to help him get a new one; he says he sees nothing wrong with the one that Igor the mailman has."

Mac stared at Anya for a moment, her eyes narrowed in thought. Anya could see there were ideas and plans churning in that busy head and she had no doubt that Mac was plotting something. Without a word, the housekeeper deliberately turned and busied herself with the bread dough; already she knew that it was better not to get involved.

The evening was chilly, and rain was threatening to arrive later during the night. Igor tiredly opened his front door, glad to finally be home. Making the deliveries on foot took a lot longer than it should; his feet were hurting, and his boots were wearing thin. He was greeted warmly by his wife and a welcoming cozy fire, a pot of stew bubbling on the stove cheered his heart. When he turned to close the front door, a cloaked figure detached itself from the shadows. As he hesitated in the doorway peering into the darkness, the hair on the back of his neck stood on end and a creepy shiver ran down his spine. The last thing he saw before slamming the door shut in alarm were gleaming eyes that glowed silver and blue from the deep recesses of a hood.

"Igor! It looks like you have seen a ghost, whatever is the matter?" His wife hurried to his side, worried and flustered.

"It is her!" The mailman swallowed hard. "*Koldun'ya* is watching us." He kept his voice lowered, whispering fearfully, not wanting to catch the attention of the witch who was lurking across the street.

Peering cautiously through the window, the two saw no sign of the terrible witch. They ate supper quietly and went to bed early, where they huddled under the covers, jumping at every sound, hoping not to be visited during the night. Later they heard strange noises coming from the back of their house, but they dared not go and investigate.

The next morning, Mailman Igor found his old bike leaning up against his garden gate, the front wheel buckled, and the handlebars bent. What could have happened to the bike was beyond him, and Komarov was just as dumbfounded. The old grouch would have blamed Igor, but for the unbelievable reports about sightings of *Koldun'ya* racing down Main Street in the middle of the night on the mailman's old rattle-trap bicycle. Komarov put the whole episode down to paranoia and dismissed the very idea that that imbecile of a girl could have had anything to do with it. After all, girls did not ride bikes, not in that fashion anyway, and it would have taken a complete lunatic to do so much damage in such a short time. Be that as it may, he felt compelled to call the girl into his office and question her on the matter.

There was a knock on the door and Sascha ushered the girl into the office. The two waited expectantly for Komarov to speak.

"McKinley." He glared sternly at the girl standing on the other side of his desk, looking for all the world like butter wouldn't melt in her mouth. This, Dimitri Komarov had learned, was a very bad sign. "What can you tell me about the mailman's bicycle?"

Unexpectedly, the girl's face lit up with a dazzling smile, her eyes sparkling with enthusiasm.

"That bicycle is not suitable for speeds over zero miles per hour. If it goes any faster, the wheels will turn and that is where the real problems start."

Sascha cleared his throat and looked fixedly down at the carpet. Dimitri Komarov could only sit and stare as the girl launched into a longwinded, totally confusing report on how the bicycle belonging to Igor the mailman performed over various tests of endurance and speed. Obstacle courses which included ramping it over stairs and sidewalks, wheelies and slides at various speeds and angles, were reported in great detail.

"After putting the bike through various rigorous tests, it became clear to me that the bike is not even suitable for the rubbish dump. That bike is so unsafe, I am sure you would never have expected your town mailman to risk his life with that bike every day, and had you known what state it was in, you would have replaced it in an instant," she concluded with a wide grin, looking at him as if she had done him a huge favor. "So that is why I decided to check it out for you."

With the old bike trashed beyond repair, and as it was his witch who was responsible, Komarov had to save face. He had no choice but to foot the bill for a brand-new bike. Mailman Igor was thrilled: his request for a new bike had eventually been heard. For over a year it had been faster, and safer to walk his routes rather than battle along with that old pile of junk, but now he was seen whipping along on a brand-new bike, whistling, his face beaming. A little trailer had also been added and it bounced along behind him, filled with items for delivery.

Sascha caught Mac standing near the window with a smile on her face, watching the mailman pedal by. His heart quickened and his stomach flipped with a deep affection for the girl. The four-year age gap between them was becoming shorter with every week that flew by. He was not far off from falling in love with this girl, and that would not do. Not at all.

Turning, she saw him watching her.

"What?" She was smiling innocently at him, her eyes gleaming with pleasure.

All he wanted to do was to pull her into his arms and kiss that delectable mouth.

"Um, good work with the scare tactics, *Koldun'ya* McKinley." He hid his feelings behind humor. "That mailman looks positively terrified."

Later that week, Sascha dropped Mac and Anya off in the middle of town. Anya needed to replenish her pantry and Mac was coming along for the ride. She was only allowed into town if she agreed to behave badly and scowl at everybody. She had to skulk behind Anya like a bad-tempered cat. No smiling! No laughing! No joking around!

On the drive to town, at first no one spoke.

"Okay." Mac glared at each in turn and her voice took on the exact tone of Mr. Dimitri's. "I do not want to see any smiles! Serious faces only. The first person to smile is the loser."

Everyone stared seriously at one another, looking for the slightest quirk. Sascha checked them in the rearview mirror...the other two stared solemnly back at him. It took just a snort of muffled laughter from Mac and everything fell apart. When they eventually drew up outside the supermarket, the three had a hard time getting into serious, terrifying mode.

As Mac and Anya moved from aisle to aisle around the shop, people kept a very wide berth, but Mac soon became aware of a group of children following at a distance. They were peeking at her through the legs of their parents and hiding behind towering tins of fish. Each time she turned around, they screamed in terror and ran, some trying to hide under the shelving. All Mac and Anya could see were little legs sticking out from various hiding places.

"*Tetya* Anya, please may I have that bag of candies?" Mac smiled at the housekeeper.

Passing the bag to Mac, Anya watched as she quietly opened it and slipped it underneath her long cloak. As she walked, the fine fabric of the cloak skimmed lightly over the floor and swirled around her feet, giving her the appearance of floating. The children watched wide-eyed as candies started appearing wherever *Koldun'ya* walked. At first, they were scared to pick the candies up: what if they were poisoned, what if it was a trap? What if the witch was wanting to plump children up so she could eat them later?

Mac stopped to look at a few books on a top shelf, watching from the corner of her eye as a small arm stretched out from behind a stack of flour bags, grubby fingers extended to the max to reach for the prize. The candy disappeared in a second, then the same arm stretched out from under the shelving a little farther down, and again the candy was snatched up in a flash. Now she was interested. Mac tracked the reaching arm as it stretched out from various hiding places plucking up the trail of candies, apples, and other treats with startling speed. Eventually the little fingers emerged at the spot where Mac was standing. They crept across the toe of her boot and then the foot. and then they froze in surprise.

A head popped out from under a table of baked goods and startled black eyes met the steady gaze of *Koldun'ya*.

"Well?" The witch looked closely at the boy, her dark eyebrows arching, her eyes gleaming from within the shadows of her hood.

"Thank you?" Peering up at the shadowed face above him, the boy marveled at the fact that he was so close to the witch and hadn't died yet.

All Mac could see were two round bright eyes in a small, round face that was pale under the dirt smudges, and a mass of spiky, matted hair.

"Are you going to come out from there?" she asked the boy.

"No, *Koldun'ya*, I think you might want to eat me."

"I most certainly would not." Mac frowned at him with her most fearsome expression. "You are not even enough for my soup bones."

The boy grinned up at her, his face lit with delight. "You are right, *Koldun'ya*. I am sure I would taste very bad."

Mac found herself wondering why this boy was so confident; why he seemed to have no real fear of the evil witch of Ivanov.

"Oh, my goodness, dear child!" Anya had come from the next aisle and was shocked to see the state of the little boy. "Where is your mother?" She reached down, took the boy's arm, and helped him to his feet. His pockets were bulging with the goods he had collected from *Koldun'ya*. His state of general neglect was obvious.

"She is sick and now we cannot wake her up. Nobody wants to help us." He had become sad and serious.

Mac looked at Anya, puzzled about why people in this town would not help a person in need.

"Come!" Anya took the child by his freezing hand. "You must be Alexei, Lenna's boy, right?" She shook her head sadly. "Let us go to your house straight away."

"We had better take food with us, Anya," Mac pointed out. "It seems that his family have nothing to eat."

As the two women hurriedly paid for the groceries and prepared to rush out of the store with the little boy, they were accosted by the shop owner.

"I will not be seen to be supporting this boy and his mother!" He grabbed Anya by the arm and wrenched her around. "The food will stay here!"

McKinley felt a rush of heat consuming her from her toes to the top of her head. Her heart pounded in her chest. How dare this man be so disrespectful! She rounded on him, her eyes glittering and blazing. She was bristling with fury.

"You will unhand Madame at once!" Her voice echoed and cracked against the walls of the building, as sharp as a whip. The shopkeeper turned, and saw *Koldun'ya*. The air around her was crackling and snapping; he could feel the force of her rage like a living, breathing dragon, writhing and spitting.

"How dare you come near us!?" She whirled around, her cloak flying about her. A crowd had gathered at the entrance of the shop. "Did any of you have the heart to help this boy? Help his family? Shame on all of you who have turned your backs on this suffering." She drew breath and seemed to grow in stature. She was so furious that she was almost levitating; many swore later that she had indeed risen off the ground.

"I am *Koldun'ya* McKinley. You have not yet witnessed my power. I have the power of the great mountains, the sleeping giants of the earth; I have the power of the earth itself. You who are at fault will live under the shadow and weight of your own pride and judgment until you find a way to do right by this family." She turned again to the shopkeeper. "And you will receive payment, much more than you expect."

Fear rendered the people speechless, their faces pale and terrified. Mac turned her back on them, slipping one arm through Anya's and the other arm around the thin shoulders of the boy. Sascha, parked out front, was leaning against the bonnet of the car, arms folded, a bemused look on his face. As they approached, he opened the doors for them, loaded the grocery bags into the car then hopped in the front seat.

"Phew, *Koldun'ya* McKinley, remind me never to get on the wrong side of you!"

Mac was still fuming. She hated the way some people treated others, as if they were better than them and had more rights. Sascha watched her in the rearview mirror and his heart swelled with admiration as he saw her eyes flashing bright and hard. Man, this girl was full of surprises. Who would have thought she had this temper on her?

Anya and the boy had been silent throughout, both awed and a little intimidated by this display. Before, Anya had just seen Mac as a sixteen-year-old girl who had found herself in strange circumstances but now, having witnessed that little lot, she wondered what Mac would be capable of when she was older. Her boss would be most pleased.

Mac noticed that Sascha did not need directions to Alexei's house. The boy seemed well known in the village, which made it even more unbelievable that nobody would help.

"What is your mother's name, Alexei?" she asked the boy.

"My mom is Lenna; she is the town prostitute," he said proudly.

"I am sorry?"

"A prostitute, you know..." He shrugged his thin shoulders. "She fixes men's clothing."

"Oh." Mac sighs, people can be such monsters.

She put her arm around the shivering boy and drew him close, wrapping him in her warm cloak.

"Here, Mr. Alexei, you look like you need some proper food in your belly." She handed him a meaty pie. "I doubt candies will help much."

Although he was literally salivating, the boy shook his head. He couldn't eat without sharing with his little brothers, he explained.

Sascha pulled over at a small house standing alone, looking dark and cold, on the outside of town. The door opened and two small boys popped their heads out.

On entering, Mac noticed that although an attempt had been made to tidy up, there were obvious signs of a struggle. The house felt strongly of fear and pain. She rushed over to a bed where a person lay huddled under thin blankets.

"Lenna," Mac whispered, leaning down to peer into the gaunt and pale face. The woman in the bed was burning up, her breathing labored and rasping.

Anya crouched next to the bed and drew the blanket down. Lenna's body was covered with dry, flakey blood, the skin discolored black and blue with vicious-looking bruises. Her leg, lying at an odd angle, was obviously broken.

"What happened to your mother?" Mac asked Alexei, who was standing worriedly at the foot of the bed along with his two younger brothers.

"We found her like this. A big man came to have his clothes fixed and she sent us to gather herbs in the field out back." Tears started trickling down the boy's grubby cheeks. "She said not to come back until she called us. We waited a long time. It was getting dark, and we were afraid, so we came home."

Anya looked up at Sascha. "Get a fire going and take the children into the kitchen. I am sure it has been far too long since they last ate.

"Alexei, go and join Sascha and your brothers in the kitchen, there is food for you and then Sascha will need help to collect wood for the fires."

Anya brought through a basin of warm water and started to clean away the grime and blood.

"We need to stabilize the leg before we can do anything else," she said. "There is no point taking her to the hospital; nobody will treat her. She is shunned in this town."

Lenna's husband had been a no-good, double-dealing crook who swindled money from the vulnerable and the foolish. He had no conscience and would target widows without a qualm. He was abusive and a drunk, and he gambled away whatever small income the family had. Lenna had tried to earn money for food by doing laundry and mending and she would do her best to hide from him the little cash she earned in this way. One night, shortly after the twins were born four years ago, Lenna's husband had just disappeared, leaving her with the three very young boys and no real means of support. When various debt collectors came knocking on her door, she had no choice but to agree to providing them with 'payment in kind'. That became how she managed to keep her house, to feed and clothe her babies and to keep her own head above water. Her dignity had been stolen by her monstrous husband years ago; now she had no pride when it came to survival, and the townsfolk turned their backs on her in judgment and disapproval.

Anya had heard some of the gossip about Lenna over the years but had thought she had moved away a while ago; now she was shocked to discover different. As Mac learned the story for the first time, she was overcome with compassion for this little family.

"She is in a lot of pain, *Tetya* Anya." Mac swallowed hard. She knew what she needed to do, but it was going to be very tough and the others could not be allowed to find out.

"I can help her." She shut the bedroom door and turned to face Anya. "But I need you to promise me that you will not tell a soul of what you are about to see, and you will not interfere, no matter how bad it looks."

Anya did not know what to think, but she nodded her agreement and continued with her work. Lenna had not come out from her restless sleep. Mac kneeled next to the bed and placed her hands on the leg. It was black and swollen, the skin almost splitting, the heat of the taut skin indicating infection and grave complications.

Mac sat back on her heels and keeping her hands firmly on the leg, she closed her eyes in concentration.

It was harsh and heavy breathing that first alerted Anya, who looked up in alarm. McKinley appeared to be in great pain. A closer look, and Anya could see lines of black and red running from the infected, broken leg, in through Mac's hands. Lenna's leg started cooling and the swelling began to dissipate, while McKinley's leg swelled up and went dark with infection. Although Mac was in excruciating pain, she did not stop, she did not lift her hands. Tears streamed down her cheeks, her harsh breathing became moans of distress. Anya could literally hear the broken bones in Lenna's leg grating together as they moved back into place and started to knit.

Anya reached out and caught McKinley just as she collapsed in a dead faint. Grabbing a pillow and blanket from the bed, she lowered her onto the floor. Now Lenna was starting to come around. Her fever had disappeared and her pain was reduced to just a faint throbbing. She was confused and bewildered, looking up at Anya with wild, panicked eyes.

"Lie still, Lenna. I am Anya, we are here to help you."

"My boys . . . where are my little ones?"

McKinley woke up a couple of hours later, finding herself lying curled on a couch. Her head throbbed and her leg hurt like the blazes. Her whole body felt battered and bruised, as if she had just gone six rounds with a bear. For some minutes, she could not think where she was. She could hear the piping voices of little children in the next room. She closed her eyes for a few more minutes, but they flew open in surprise when a small, warm, sticky hand pressed against her cheek and soft little lips kissed her gently on her forehead. She opened her eyes to see the concerned face of a little boy, his round cheeks flushed and smeared with gravy.

"*Tetya* Kinley," he whispered. 'You alive?"

Swallowing hard, she nodded. Her throat was as dry and parched as the Atacama Desert. Another little face appeared in her field of vision, identical to the other. He leaned in close and looked into her eyes, his little forehead furrowed in concentration. He stared for a few moments, then he too kissed her gently on the forehead before turning to his brother.

"God ran out."

"He ran out?"

"Sure, so He had to use another crayon."

Both little faces leaned down again. Squinting, the boys looked closely into Mac's eyes, studying first the blue then the gray with intense focus. The little boys were completely absorbed with the puzzle of Mac's odd eyes.

"Do they see different?" The question was whispered reverently.

"What?" Mac's voice was hoarse, and her parched throat grated like a piece of sandpaper.

"You know… can one see in the dark, and one see in the light?"

"Does only the one see colors?"

Mac stared up into the chubby little faces looking down at her so seriously, and she started laughing – well, tried to laugh anyway; it turned instead into a coughing fit.

"Oh no, you two! What are you doing?" A horrified voice came from the doorway.

The two little boys whirled around. The guilt written on their faces was too much for Mac and she ended up gasping for breath.

Their mother, Lenna, came into the room and ushered the two mini-scientists out. Lenna moved stiffly with a slight limp, but she was up and about.

"My Lady! I do apologize. I told them not to disturb you. I am so glad you are awake." She was relieved to see the witch was recovering.

"Sascha and Anya had to return to the master's house. Sascha will be along later to fetch you."

Lenna fussed around Mac, propping her up against pillows, then she brought Mac a bowl of soup with thick slices of dark bread.

"Lenna." Mac looked up at the young woman intently. "Please, nobody needs to know of what happened here today."

Lenna stared at Mac for a moment, her dark eyes narrowed, her mouth twisted in a bitter smile.

"My Lady, you have no need to worry. No one knows about being used and abused more than I."

"You are no longer alone, Lenna. You have *Koldun'ya* McKinley for a friend and you have *Tetya* Anya and Sascha too."

Sascha could not understand why Mac had fainted; he was sure that the women were not telling him the whole story. He had carried her to the couch in the lounge, and he had noticed her many injuries. How had she become so bruised and beaten? Surely it was not just because she had collapsed onto the floor. How come Lenna had made such a miraculous recovery? Nothing made a bit of sense and getting the truth from these women was like trying to wring water from a desert rock. There was no way they would talk. Maybe he should try the little ones, they should spill the beans with the right leverage. Anya was very quiet on the way back to the mansion, and on arriving she went straight into the kitchen and started with supper preparations. Luckily the boss was busy with paperwork and conference calls; he would not be happy to learn that his witch had been left at the house of the town whore.

By the time Sascha arrive to fetch Mac, it was already dark. He found her fully recovered, sitting at the kitchen table entertaining three very lively little boys. He had heard their shouts of laughter and excited conversation way before he even knocked on the door. Lenna let him into the house, shaking her head in disbelief, a bemused smile on her face. Yup, that was a normal expression for a person to have, after just a few minutes in McKinley's crazy company.

"Oh, my goodness!" Lenna exclaimed. "Where on earth does she come up with this stuff?"

"I have learned it is best not to ask, it is easier to just go with the flow." Sascha grinned.

Chapter 6 – Trouble Personified

Sitting at his desk, Dimitri Komarov is surrounded by an endless mountain of paperwork. He stares at the three people gathered in his office for the usual morning meeting, who are waiting respectfully for him to speak. (Well. . . mostly respectful.) It has been four years since the witch joined his household and he still can never be sure what she is about to do next. At nineteen, she is just as much trouble. . . actually, even more so . . . than when she was younger. He has had to think outside the box to keep her mind occupied with things besides making mischief and causing mayhem in the town. His suggestion that she try writing her own books has kept her sufficiently busy for now. He had, of course, had to get her a laptop to work from. If he had known that having a witch would be so much trouble, he would have thought twice, but to be totally honest, he really cannot imagine life without her now. She has brought a joyful madness and much laughter into his household, something he had long forgotten about. If he had ever had a daughter, this would be her. Of course, he will never let on to anyone of his fondness for the girl; that would just not do. But his house feels as if it holds a family again, as if it is no longer just an empty shell.

Once a year he has allowed Mac to go home to visit her own family. Every time that she is away, everyone in his household and in the town seems to sink into a depression until she returns. On the day of her arrival, there is always an atmosphere of celebration: laughter echoes once more in the streets, and the town seems to lift out of a dark slump and once again becomes hopeful and vibrant.

"McKinley."

Dimitri Komarov is looking at his witch now with his usual stern and irritated expression.

"You are to take some self-defense lessons. Sascha will instruct you."

"Self-defense?" Mac looks at Mr. Dimitri closely. "But I am a witch – what self-defense would I need?" Then her eyes light up and she grins at him. He and the other two brace themselves for what she is about to say; it is guaranteed to be something outrageous and cheeky.

"Oh, I get it. Defense against the dark arts? I have read about that." Then she frowns, and turns to looks at Sascha who involuntarily takes a step back.

"You know about that stuff?" She considers him through narrowed eyes. "I thought we needed wands to do that type of thing... and I told you what happened to my w…"

"No problem, boss." Sascha hurriedly cuts across Mac's words. He knows what she is about to say, and it is bound to irritate the boss beyond all reason.

"Good." The boss mutters, he eyes Mac with a steely look, daring her to say something more. But she doesn't say a word, she just stands there grinning widely at him, a picture of innocence.

"Right, meeting over, you can all get out now." Komarov can only take this girl in small doses, and right now he is way above his limit.

When Dimitri Komarov was a much younger man he lost his family to the strife and upheaval of a changing world. He refuses to dwell on those dark times but he has become hard and closed off, without an ounce of compassion for the suffering of others. He promised himself many years back that he would not allow another living thing to get close to his heart again; he never again wants to feel that shattering of his heart, that exploding of his soul as his life is ripped to shreds.

It has taken a while for McKinley to break those walls down and to creep into his heart. In those first months, the girl irritated him beyond all reason so much so, that on more than one occasion he would have happily throttled her. Occasions such as the time when she dared come home with outfits that were not at all what he had wanted Madame to make. Not the cape he had envisioned, nor the narrow, long skirts, and no straight hair. What was Madame thinking? He had spent long hours on the internet, studying all the various witch outfits, and he had found the perfect style. All that effort down the toilet; all that time wasted. When he confronted the dressmaker, the woman merely shrugged and told him that: "*Koldun'ya* McKinley could not climb trees, jump over walls or onto rooftops in a long dress." And had then added, "Good luck with making *Koldun'ya* McKinley do anything that she does not want to."

But Mac's impish smile, that hopelessly naughty face, and her constantly busy mind began to wear on Komarov's ridged heart and crack his impenetrable, invincible walls. Nowadays, he chases the three incorrigibles out of his office not because he has had enough of them, but because he is battling to keep his face straight and his scowl in place.

Sascha does not waste any time, and the self-defense lesson starts as soon as they have changed into suitable clothing. There is of course a fully equipped gym at the back of the house which he uses daily. Sascha is fluent in all the martial arts as well as in everyday street fighting with all the related weapons. He starts by showing Mac some basic moves and blocks. At first, he is impressed at how fast she is picking it up, then he starts to get suspicious of just how much Mac really knows when in no time he finds that the roles have reversed and he is having to defend himself against her. She is fast, strong, and cunning. She catches him off guard and he finds himself being flung down onto the mat with Mac sitting on top of him, her eyes shining with mischief and laughter.

"You have done this before, you little cheat." Sascha's silver eyes gleam back at her.

"I didn't cheat," she scoffs. "You guys just assumed that a girl knows nothing - typical!"

She leans down, smiling, her face very close to his. She looks him in the eye.

"So do you give up?"

He moves so fast that before Mac has a chance to draw breath, she is on her back with Sascha pinning her to the mat.

"Do you?" He looks down at her, laughter lighting his face.

Gazing into her shining eyes, Sascha is overcome with feelings that he cannot afford to feel. His hurried attempt to get off her and back onto his feet, is foiled by Mac as she grabs the front of his t-shirt.

"Sasch. . ." She is out of breath, smiling at him. Her face has 'naughty' written all over it. He swallows hard.

"Sasch, will you kiss me again? This time leave out the finger-kissing part, you don't need to test my waters."

"Not a good idea, Mac." But he is staring at her lips. She pulls him closer.

"I promise I won't slap you." She smiles. "I know you won't slobber all over me."

"And how can you be so sure about that, Miss McKinley?" Sascha's smile is not quite reaching his eyes. His attempt at being light-hearted is betrayed by that very heart crashing heavily against his ribs, as if it is trying to escape his chest to get to Mac's heart.

"Awww, c'mon Sasch, just do it." Her smile has also slipped a bit; her heart too is hammering slightly too hard.

Then, against his better judgment, and totally ignoring that wise inner voice that is literally screaming for him to stop, he lowers his mouth onto hers.

The minute Sascha's lips find hers, McKinley's insides turn to liquid fire, raging up from the pit of her stomach, expanding and overwhelming her entirely. She slides her hands up his arms, she feels his hot, smooth skin, she feels the hard muscles flexing under her hands. With her arms around his neck, she pulls him closer, trying to feel every inch of his hard body against hers. She cannot seem to get close enough. She needs to be a part of him; she wants to climb inside him. A wave of frustration has her clinging to him, and once again she is overcome with feelings that are too complicated, too much. Her brain once again has turned to mush. Fiery emotion has flooded her body – uncontained, wild, and thrilling.

Sascha is having a problem getting himself under control. His blood is surging, scorching hot in his veins, as he feels her slight, supple body against his. Phew, McKinley! She has no reservation. She has no filter, no off button. Everything she does has to be at full blast. Kissing her is like playing with a stick of dynamite. She does nothing in half measures and is demanding that he do the same. He has got to find strength; he needs to put on the brakes before all control is lost. With desperate effort, Sascha raises his head. Their eyes meet.

"Wow!" Mac's eyes are glowing, her face flushed. "That is nowhere near how the books tell it." Then she frowns accusingly at Sascha who is hastily getting to his feet, taking deep, calming breaths.

"Are you sure you did that right?"

"What?" He reaches down and pulls Mac to her feet.

"Well, for one, I can't see how anyone can survive it for too long, I think my heart would have just exploded if you hadn't stopped just then."

"Well, *Koldun'ya* McKinley . . ." Sascha cannot help laughing at the workings of her crazy and outrageous mind. "I guess now you are going to just have to spend sleepless nights wondering: 'Did he do it right, or didn't he? Would my heart really have exploded?'"

"Oh." She sounds disappointed. "I don't want to spend sleepless nights wondering that. Would you give it another shot now? Just to make sure?"

Shaking his head, Sascha picks his jacket up and moves toward the door. "I think that is enough training for one day, Mac." He turns to face her.

"Your magic is far too strong for me, McKinley." His silver eyes are serious for once. "I am afraid that next time there will be no stopping, and then my heart will be well beyond saving."

Two days later, Dimitri Komarov watches as the three file out of his office. His witch is in fine fettle this morning and her snappy come-backs did not disappoint. From the time four years ago that McKinley entered like an uncontainable hurricane into everyone's lives, there have been incidents around town that Komarov cannot ignore. After Mailman Igor managed to get a new bicycle, others have also had their wishes fulfilled.

Among many small incidents, there are some that have stood out – like the time that the school finally got decent renovations done, even acquiring a new roof. Komarov will never forget it. Nobody could fathom how Farmer Novikov's old tractor managed to get wedged in the doorway of that old derelict building. When it was finally removed, half the brick-work and the whole doorframe came away with it. That caused some of the roof to collapse. Of course, *Koldun'ya* McKinley was to blame. Of course, there were witnesses who swore they saw her hanging on for dear life as she went roaring down the road on that broken-down heap of scrap, at times bouncing right out of her seat, a huge grin on her face. With the engine protesting wildly, back-firing and spurting black smoke all the way. Many questions crowd into Komarov's mind. Foremost is how the heck his witch succeeded in starting that useless piece of outdated machinery, and how on earth does she even know how to drive a tractor? That little episode put him out of pocket by a massive amount. Not only did he have to pay for the long-overdue renovations on the school building that he just happened to own, but he also had to replace the tractor. Old Farmer Novikov had been coming to him for years asking for help to replace that tractor of his, and Komarov always found some reason to refuse the request. Then suddenly there was no choice but to buy the farmer another tractor. Mmmm....... coincidence? Dimitri Komarov thinks not.

There was the time when she was just a young girl and she gave the whole community a dressing down for not helping the town whore. With disbelief, he heard the stories of how his witch became a voice of power; she had cursed the whole lot of them. Not long after that, the shopkeeper was horrified to find that his customers had dwindled to a trickle; everyone was far too scared to support a business that had been so publicly cursed. It hasn't escaped Komarov that Lenna and her three boys are now seen walking in town, all smartly dressed, respectful and respected. Lenna has found work with Madame Tarasova, the dressmaker, and has moved into a lovely little cottage on the right side of town. She is no longer visited by anyone but genuine friends and she has somehow gained quite a lot of those. Because it is public knowledge that she is under the protection of the Ivanov Witch, she has nothing to fear from anyone.

Somehow the requests of all the townsfolk are being granted, one way or another. It also hasn't escaped Komarov's notice that the town is starting to bloom and prosper. Not just the town, but he is not doing too badly himself. He managed to buy the General Store cheaply; he has been after that business for years. These days, people are treating him with much greater respect and with a loyalty that does not come from a place of fear, but a place of genuine admiration.

His thoughts are interrupted by a tap on the door. Oh good, that must be Anya with the coffee.

"Come!" Komarov uses his stern voice.

"Sorry, sir, there is a man downstairs to see you." The housekeeper sounds flustered and worried.

"Name?"

"Borya Komarov. He says he is your brother."

Komarov's heart stops for a moment and then continues at a rapid rate. He can feel all the blood drain from his face.

"Anya, please show the man into the library. Tell him that I will be down shortly."

Before the housekeeper disappears, he calls her back.

"Please find Sascha. He must make sure that any thugs accompanying my brother, stay outside the house along with all weapons."

As the housekeeper disappears through the doorway, he slumps back in his chair. Taking his handkerchief from his pocket, he mops the sweat from his face. Borya. He is the last person that Komarov expected to see, the last person in the world he wants to see. The man is a snake. Just two years older, Borya has been a blight in the life of Komarov from the day he was born. Mean, self-serving, conniving, and vindictive, the man has no limits when it comes to wealth and personal gain. He would slit the throat of his own son without a thought to get what he wants. Luckily, he has no family. Just Dimitri.

Komarov checks his own weapon and places it in a holster, in plain sight. As he makes his way down the stairs, he hears his brother's voice coming from the library. Exasperated and furious, edging beyond control. Oh no! Is Mac in the library? Komarov is about to rush into the library, when his man Sascha steps forward.

"Maybe we should leave him with Mac just a few minutes more?" Sascha is smiling, his eyes bright.

"My brother will have either strangled Mac by then, or hanged himself," Komarov mutters as he edges toward the door.

Anya comes out of the kitchen to find both Komarov and Sascha standing with their ears pressed against the door, with gleeful smiles on their faces.

"What on earth?"

"Shhh…." Sascha nods toward the library. "Mac is in there,"

Anya's uncertainty clears and with gleaming eyes and a grin on her face, she too presses her ear against the door.

Chapter 7 – She Would Never!

Yes, indeed. *Koldun'ya* McKinley is in the library; she is in there whenever she has a chance. She couldn't believe the number of books just sitting there on the shelves. Starting from one side, she has been making her way along the shelves. She is determined to read every book in this room and she only has the back wall to complete now. Shouldn't take long.

Today, Mac is absorbed in the complicated lives of the Ancient Greeks. Goodness, how on earth had they managed to do anything at all, with the gods constantly interfering with their lives? She is dragged back to reality by the raised voice of a stranger coming from the hallway. She can hear the calm voice of Sascha too, as he firmly but politely shows the man into the library. Neither of them notices her sitting in her favorite squishy chair near the fire.

"I will not be treated in such a way! I demand to see my brother immediately." The voice is hard with rough, bitter edges. Mac feels the hair rise up on the back of her neck. If this man has a heart at all, it is black and dead.

"Mr. Komarov will be with you shortly." Sascha walks out of the library, leaving the visitor to continue with his ranting alone.

"If that imbecile brother of mine thinks he can hide in this backwoods, he has another think coming." The man storms around the room. "How dare he make me wait, like some infernal servant!"

The man makes his way to where the large fire is blazing. How dare his brother be so comfortable and how dare he own such lavish possessions. . .

He stops in mid-rant as he rounds the chair and comes face to face with … with … he has no idea what to think. A girl, sitting in an armchair that is so big it is almost swallowing her whole. If he was imaginative or even whimsical – which he most certainly is not – he would swear that this person can only have materialized straight out of one of those useless fairytale books.

"And just who are you?" Borya Komarov demands.

Unshaken by his most hard and angry glare, a glare that normally has grown men quaking in fear, the person in the chair looks up with a lofty gaze. Her impudence is written on her face as plain as day.

"I was about to ask you the same thing." Her tone is frosty and diminishing. She does not bother to stand, neither does she bother answering his question. She continues to stare at him with those unsettling odd eyes, her fine brows raised in question.

Huffing and puffing with disbelief, Borya feels heat rising to his scanty hairline. He cannot believe the audacity.

"Well?" She has now laid her book down, giving him the full brunt of a haughty stare, obviously fully expecting him to reply.

By this time, Borya's eyes are bugging out with rage and frustration. The huffing and puffing have become louder and his face has turned beet red.

"I will not be treated in such a way." He is spitting.

"You look like you need to calm down; I know just the trick. I find that reading makes one calm almost instantly. Do you read?

I love reading. I have read all these books, starting from this shelf. I will tell you all about them one at a time. Please let me know if you do not understand; you do not look very clever – do you even know how to read?"

McKinley has been unleashed, and she is taking full advantage. Without seeming to pause for breath, she launches into detailed descriptions of each book. Of course, as she had done years previously, she makes most of the stuff up and her stories become more and more ludicrous, so entangled that even the most intelligent person in the world would not be able to follow the storylines.

At first, Borya is speechless, taken by surprise by the overbearing and insulting barrage of words flowing from the mouth of this unbelievably irritating girl. He does not miss the bold underlying theme that portrays him as the imbecile of each story that she launches into. Borya is beside himself. How dare this girl speak to him with such disrespect? How dare she speak to him at all? She has effectively cut him down and rendered him speechless. He feels like he needs to smash something. Whirling around, he goes to grab a glass bowl from the table but before he takes one step, without missing a beat, she stops him short.

"I wouldn't do that."

"What?!" How does she know what he is going to do?

"You came here to trash your brother's library?" Now she is speaking to him as if he – the great and terrifying Borya Komarov – is but a naughty little boy.

Mac leans back in her chair. Placing her steepled fingers against her chin, she regards Borya through narrowed eyes.

Borya splutters uselessly. He has never in his life been treated this way, with such casual indifference. He stands rooted to the floor, with a thousand thoughts whirling through his head. He feels a strong need to run from the room; he also would love to just throw himself right through the window … or even better, throw the girl through the window. He wants to shout at her to stop; even to plead and beg. As he stares down at the girl curled so comfortably in that chair, his blood feels like it has started to boil, sweat drips from his temples, and his breathing is starting to come in heaving gasps.

"Borya, so sorry to keep you." His brother enters the library. The atmosphere that has built up in that room between himself and the girl is so thick that Borya could almost hear it tearing apart, like cloth being ripped, dissipating as Komarov makes his appearance.

"For goodness' sake!" Borya swings around to face his brother. "You need to do something about this girl."

"Who . . . Mac?" Komarov raises his eyebrows in surprise, his expression dumbfounded. Mac immediately catches on and she jumps to her feet, a picture of total respect.

"Good day, Mr. Komarov, sir." She turns to Dimitri and bows as if to a king. "I hope your day is going well, sir. Would you like me to organize some tea?"

"Thank you, Mac, but tea will not be necessary."

Borya cannot believe what he is witnessing. The change in the girl is astounding. Just as she is about to exit the room, she turns and looks him up and down with complete disdain.

"There! You see? No manners! If she were mine, I would have beaten her senseless."

"Certainly not! I have no idea what you are talking about, Borya. Mac shows nothing but great respect and superb manners." Komarov moves to the drinks table and pours out two glasses. Handing one to his brother, he moves to the fire. "Now, what can I do for you?"

"Can a man not visit his brother?" Borya smirks.

"Not if that man is you, Borya. You know there is no welcome for you here."

Borya narrows his eyes, his fingers tightening on his glass. "You have changed, Dimitri. What is giving you all this confidence? Could it be a change in your household?"

"I do not know what you are talking about. We are no longer children; we have made our own lives."

"And I see you have done very well for yourself – a little too well." Borya watches his brother over his glass.

"Stop playing, Borya. Say what you need to say. I have not the time nor the patience for games."

"I have come to see if all the stories are true . . . I have come to see your witch."

"My witch?" Komarov chokes in mid-swallow.

"You do have a witch, don't you?" Borya approaches and stands next to his brother.

"What have you heard about my witch?"

"It is well known; your witch is a weapon of death and destruction."

"Um, she is?" Komarov frowns, then nods. "She is a lot of trouble."

"Of course, how else would you have been able to build your wealth this way?"

Komarov realizes that his brother has no idea what the Witch of Ivanov even looks like. He is fishing for information like the sly snake that he is. Komarov is briefly tempted to let his monster of a brother take his witch; it would be very satisfying to see the man driven mad with frustration and confusion.

"She is not here. She is a free spirit; she comes and goes as she pleases." Komarov swallows the contents of his glass. "There is no power on this earth that can force her to do anything that she does not want to do."

That sounds exactly the sort of challenge that Borya finds irresistible. Putting his empty glass down, he changes the subject, feigning a loss of interest.

The weather has turned foul and the roads out of Ivanhof have been closed. As his brother and entourage are now stranded, manners force Komarov to act as the gracious host and put the uninvited guests up in his house. Anya has Mac and Sascha help with making up the rooms while she sets about preparing an elaborate meal.

Sascha is not too pleased at being stuck with McKinley, making beds. He cannot be near her without thinking of those soft lips, that body melting against his. He has tried to keep his distance; not easy when she is like a magnet to him, when the attraction is so strong and he is helpless to the pull.

Mac cannot understand Sascha's sudden coolness toward her. She misses her friend; she misses the easiness between them. She cannot deny that she wouldn't mind another of his demonstrations on kissing. Just the thought of it, rekindles the flames in the pit of her stomach and quickens her heart.

When she opens the door to the first guest room, Sascha follows her in with the freshly-laundered bedding.

"Okay, Sasch," she says bossily. "You stand on the other side of the bed. If we work as a team, we will get this done in record time."

As they lay down the fitted sheet, Mac purposely flicks it out of Sascha's hands. Her face is full of mischief. He grins and throws a pillow at her. She promptly catches the pillow, jumps up onto the bed and whacks him across his middle. Sascha grabs the other pillow and hits her right on the butt. And the fight is on.

Down in the library, the Komarov brothers are steadily working their way through a bottle of vodka. Shouts, curses, and loud thumps can be heard coming from an upstairs room.

"What in the world.......?" Borya stares up at the ceiling.

"Oh, don't mind that." Komarov is certain that whatever it is that is happening upstairs, Mac is involved. He keeps his face serious. "It is just the help, making up your rooms."

Upstairs, the fight is in full swing. Now Sascha and McKinley are both standing on the bed, each trying to get in a good whack. Their pillows are in a sorry state and both are gasping, struggling to master their breathless laughter. Mac loses her balance on the precarious footing of the mattress and bounces off the bed to land on the carpeted floor. Sascha reaches out, trying to save her, and ends up getting pulled off the bed after her. He lands on top of her.

"Ooof, sorry, Mac." He laughs.

Mac reaches out from under him and manages to grab a pillow from the bed, but the angle is all wrong and her attempted hit ends up with the pillow flying over their heads.

"You are such a wicked little cheat, McKinley." Sascha shakes his head, trying to contain his laughter. As he stands up, he pulls her up with him, but Mac is far from finished with this man. She pushes him back against the wall and, without pause, she leans up and plants a big juicy kiss right on his lips. Then another, on his cheeks. And on his eyelids. As she moves her mouth back to his, all laughter has ceased. His hand moves to the back of her head and, threading his fingers through her silky hair, he keeps her mouth captive on his. His lips move against hers.

At first, Mac was only playing with Sascha. She was tired of his aloofness, tired of him avoiding her at every chance. But her plan to show him that he needn't be afraid of her kisses, backfires as badly as Farmer Novikov's old rust-bucket tractor. Instead of keeping the mood light and humorous, it has fast turned into fiery blood, crashing hearts, and clutching fingers.

"I just can't stop kissing you, Sasch," Mac whispers against his mouth. "You are like a drug to me."

"Are you two finished up there? I am needing help in the kitchen!" The voice of Anya calling from the bottom of the stairs cuts through the fireworks and smoke.

The two jerk guiltily apart and they stare at each other for a few lingering seconds, their breath coming in heaving gasps. Sascha keeps a hold of his McKinley; he never wants to let her go, she has his heart and soul and he wants hers in return. She is staring at him, her face completely serious. In place of the sparkle and shine of laughter and mischief, there is a deeper glow, a shimmering that flickers darkly in her eyes.

"*Tetya* Anya is looking for us." It is all she can think to say, the only thing that can get past all the rampaging feelings that are clogging her mind and swelling her heart. She understands now why Sascha has been keeping his distance. All she wants is to stay in his arms, to feel his skin under her fingers, to feel his heart beating with hers. Phew! This has just become extremely complicated.

Komarov knows that Borya is as dangerous, cunning and relentless as a hungry polar bear on the hunt, and that his brother is after his witch, It is important that Mac is not let out of sight. They need to keep her safe.

Mac helps Anya with serving the meal. Mr. Dimitri had insisted that she wear one of those ridiculous servant outfits, with her long hair bundled up and hidden under one of those silly caps. Anya has told her that she must keep her eyes lowered as much as possible; that she should say and do nothing that will bring attention to herself. The boss wants the evening to run smoothly, to get it over and done with.

When Mac and Anya enter the dining room with platters of roast meat, the men's lewd and rude comments make her lift her head, her eyes shooting angry sparks. She 'accidently' tips the whole hot and steaming platter into the lap of the loudest and most mocking blockhead. Ooops. . . sorry about the gravy being tipped onto the head of the dweeb who is most demeaning and crude. Oh, excuse me, you big oaf, while I slosh this strong, black coffee onto your very smart dinner shirt.

By the time the dessert course comes around, all the remaining men are the picture of good manners; well-behaved and extremely polite. Sascha had been told to be at the dinner, and both he and

Komarov have been grinning like Cheshire cats throughout the entire meal. Although Komarov was not at all pleased about the way Mac was drawing attention to herself, the entertainment she provided was well worth it. Borya, of course, was huffing and puffing throughout, complaining bitterly about the infernal clumsiness of this street urchin of a girl.

After the dinner, the guests disappear into the library for smokes and drinks. Sascha joins Mac and Anya in the kitchen. They set about cleaning up, and as usual the conversation soon becomes rowdy and animated. Mac's outrageous comments and outlandish imitations of all those men around the table, have Anya and Sascha in fits of laughter.

"So, what did 'Coffee Guy' do to deserve his shirt being permanently ruined?" asks Anya, wiping the tears from her eyes.

"That guy?" Mac scoffs. "His hands were all over the place!"

"No way, Mac." Sascha is not at all pleased. Words and looks are one thing, but another man daring to put his hands on McKinley? That is so not on. "I will kill him! What did he do?"

"You want me to show you?" Mac smiles innocently.

"Will I need to pour coffee over you?"

"Probably." She laughs.

McKinley would not mind putting her hands on Sascha right now . . . nope, she wouldn't mind one bit.

The following morning the house is as quiet as a grave. There is no humming or whistling, no cheerful banter, no activity. Anya popped her head into Mac's room earlier, where she could just make out the shape of her in the dim light of dawn, curled up, fast asleep. Anya thought it unusual that the girl was still asleep, but the evening before had been busy and it was well after midnight until they had all fallen into bed. She decided to let the girl sleep for a while longer. But that was an hour ago, and there is still no movement anywhere near Mac's room. Popping her head in again, Anya calls out. No reply. She moves to the bedside; everything is suspiciously still. Throwing back the covers, she sees that pillows have been stuffed under the blankets and Mac is nowhere in sight.

Chapter 8 – A Witch? More Like A Demon From Hell

McKinley wakes up lying curled on her side, with a thumping headache. She has no clue where she is. The darkness is so thick around her that she is not even sure that her eyes are open. The pressure she feels over her eyes and around her head suggests a blindfold. Her mouth has been painfully gagged with a piece of cloth that tastes of the blood oozing from a cut on her lower lip. At least, that is what it feels like. She surely has one of those hessian feed sacks over her head; she cannot breathe properly. The air around her is moist and smells strongly of dirt and mold. Her hands are tightly bound behind her back, and her feet are tied up just as firmly. Is she inside some kind of box? She cannot straighten her legs; she cannot lift her head. Feeling increasingly claustrophobic, the urge to panic is strong and almost overwhelms her.

"Stop, Mac." The voice of her Pops sounds loud and clear in her head. "You must calm yourself; slow your breathing, use your senses. Gather as much information as you can. Prepare yourself."

The sudden memory hits her with such clarity, she feels as if she is six again. A little girl trapped in the bottom of an old well. She had fallen through the rotten boards covering the hole and had been stuck for hours. The sound of her father's voice, the sight of his smiling face appearing in the opening above her like the angel she knew him to be, split the darkness that is now crowding in on her like a shroud. Luckily for six-year-old McKinley, the well had been just deep enough to trap a little girl, the walls just sheer and slippery enough to stop the unstoppable Mac from escaping her forced imprisonment. Her Pops made sure that she was unhurt and then he helped her to help herself, showing her some techniques she could use to overcome the slippery walls of the well. She escaped using her own willpower and strength, emerging from that hole into his waiting arms. He shouted with joy and praise, wrapping his strong arms around her, hugging her to his solid chest. He lifted her up onto his broad shoulders and took her home, riding high and proud. Mac remembers the exhilaration of accomplishment. Although she was exhausted, she was not defeated.

McKinley feels her Pops close to her now. She hears his voice, calm and encouraging. Taking breaths as deep as she can manage, she opens her senses to her surroundings. Total darkness; not a glimmer of light. The faint scent of cigar smoke, mixed with a mechanical smell of fuel vapors, finds its way through the overpowering odors of the bag covering her head; the stench of dank rooms and rot. There is a hum and a drone of an engine, a constant vibration, and occasionally she is bumped around. Has she been stuffed into the trunk of a car? Really?

Mac thinks back. One of the last things she remembers is the dinner party held for that revolting man Borya and his six equally revolting men.

She remembers cleaning up with *Tetya* Anya and Sascha, and they had all gone off to bed shortly after that. With the kitchen finally spotless, and the lateness of the hour, their beds beckoned.

She remembers now that as she walked into her room, the door clicked shut behind her, leaving her in total darkness. Hating shut doors and closed-up rooms, she swung around to open it. That was when strong arms grabbed her roughly from behind and held her captive while a foul, strong-smelling cloth was pressed against her nose and mouth. As much as she tried to struggle and to shout out, it only took a few seconds before she felt her body go limp and everything went black.

Mac does not know how long she was unconscious nor how long she has been lying in this cramped trunk. She does not even know if it is day or night. She tries her bonds but they are expertly tied, almost too tight; the tips of her fingers are feeling icy and tingling from insufficient circulation. That is the least of her problems. Besides her head feeling as if it is about to crack open, her legs and arms are cramping badly from the containment and the angle at which they have been bound. Every muscle in her body is in spasm, screaming for release. Above all that, she is busting to use the bathroom. How long she can hold onto her complaining bladder is anyone's guess. She cannot move to attract attention; it will just make things a lot worse.

It seems like an eternity before the vehicle eventually comes to a halt. She can hear the hurried crunching of footsteps and the hum of muffled voices above a hard drumming sound on top of the trunk. A key scrapes in the lock and the trunk opens. Immediately, she is hit by a blast of icy rain that is driven and whipped by gale-force wind. The freezing rain pelts down, drenching her within seconds, soaking the bag that is covering her head, causing it to cling to her face. She cannot breathe; it feels as if she is drowning. McKinley starts panicking and struggling, her urgent need to use the bathroom long forgotten in her fight for air.

"Get her out of there before we all freeze to death!" a man shouts from a short distance away. Rough hands grab her arms and haul her out of the trunk. Her muscles immediately cramp up in protest, turning into concrete. With blood flowing more freely into her extremities, comes unbelievable pain. Her whole body is now on fire. The revival of her nerve-endings brings involuntary movement, and her arms and legs jerk spasmodically. But now that she is upright Mac can breathe more freely, and some fresh air seeps in under the sodden sack. Her legs buckle and she knows she would collapse into the freezing mud if it were not for the men standing either side of her, their fingers digging into the flesh of her arms. One of the men lifts her up and hefts her over his shoulder like a sack of potatoes and they all run for cover.

Luckily the distance is short. The man hurries through a doorway, knocking Mac's head against the side, then dumps her unceremoniously down at his feet. Her eyes are smarting from the knock on her head and the harsh, cutting pain of her frozen body landing on a hard floor. Although the room is dry, it is still mind-numbingly cold. She remains in complete darkness, her limbs in the clutches of burning pain, her clothes soaked with iced water. She has never in her life felt this cold; so cold that that it feels as if her skin is on fire.

"Are you sure you have the right woman?"

Mac recognizes the voice. Borya Komarov – the snake.

"The man in the village told us exactly which room was hers. He had to do repairs to her fireplace once."

"Did she fit the description that he gave you?"

There is an uncomfortable silence and a shuffling of feet.

"The villagers would not speak. Information on the witch was not easy to get. Her room location and a vague description were the only details we could get from anyone."

"What are you talking about?" Borya's voice is tight with irritation and impatience.

"The townsfolk are extremely protective and respectful of their witch; nobody will utter a word against her. She is believed to be very powerful."

"Good, good." Borya sounds more pleased. "Then they won't mind paying what I ask to get her back."

Mac hears approaching footsteps above the chattering of her teeth. Now her whole body is wracked with fits of shivering. She feels the need to throw up.

"Take her to the back room. Make sure it is fully secured before you loosen her bonds."

"Loosen her bonds? Will that be wise?"

"Do not question me, imbecile!" The words are followed by a sharp smack.

Despite her untold discomfort, Mac rolls her eyes. Borya Komarov: what a moronic dolt.

"Now, just take her there. I want Dr. Tatts to check her."

As Mac is hefted once more over a shoulder, the bag falls off her head and her hair sweeps down in all its black and white splendor.

"You have got to be kidding me!" A muttered oath. "Stop!"

Rapid footsteps approach and a hand yanks her head up by the hair and pulls down her blindfold. Glittering eyes, rich blue and silver-gray, meet those of Borya, with a malice that slams fear directly into his heart. This girl is straight from his nightmares; he feels as if he is looking down on his destruction.

"You!"

Borya releases her roughly, and swings around to face his men.

"Who is responsible for bringing this evil into my home?"

They look at one another, puzzled beyond comprehension. Has their boss gone completely mad? Had he not wanted them to bring this *Koldun'ya* of Ivanov to his house? Had he not ordered them on this mission? The man who has Mac draped over his shoulder turns and addresses his boss, with great trepidation.

"It is I, sir. I am the one who captured *Koldun'ya*."

By now the other men have ventured closer. The bedroom belonging to *Koldun'ya* had been dark at the time of the kidnapping; from the doorway, Mac was just a silhouette. They had not noticed her eyes, which were closed in a drugged sleep while they carried her quietly out of the house and manhandled her into the trunk of one of the cars. All they had noticed was her startling hair coloring, hair that had been hidden from them under a cap during dinner. That had been the only description of her that they could get out of anyone; obviously the fact that her eyes don't match was not something the villagers had wanted to impart.

Borya stands to one side and once again pulls Mac's head up by her hair. Her eyes are still blazing with the need to do bodily harm. She glares at each man in turn. Although she is still gagged, her odd-colored eyes speak volumes and they understand her intentions loud and clear. mostly having to do with administering pain; a lot of pain.

"She is the witch? The serving girl?" The men are amazed and confused.

"No, you idiots!" Borya is fuming. "This is no witch! This is a demon straight from hell." He turns on his heel. "Just make sure you do not remove that gag from her mouth, or she will drive us all to our deaths." He strides away, and disappears through the doorway.

Chapter 9 – Meanwhile, Back At The Ranch

"**M**ac is gone!"
"*Koldun'ya* McKinley has been stolen!"

The town is abuzz with panic and shock. How can this be? How can anyone do this to their darling? To their girl? An underlying wave of anger and frustration ripples through the town. Talk of rescue and revenge is rife. A crowd of vigilantes has gathered at Dimitri Komarov's front door – a huge crowd; the whole town has gathered there, demanding to know what Komarov is going to do about it. News that their witch is in the hands of Komarov's brother has done the rounds and they are baying for blood. How dare someone just come in and take their witch? How dare they even think about it?

Anya has not stopped crying. A note had been delivered early on the morning following Mac's disappearance: Pay up or else. A lock of her beautiful hair was included. The price for her safe return is exorbitant, far more than anyone including Dimitri Komarov can afford.

Sascha is in a turmoil. He is furious with himself. He is responsible for the security of the house; how had his Mac been spirited away, right under his nose? He is furious also with Borya Komarov, at his audacity and conniving greed. Most of all he has a gut-wrenching fear for Mac. His heart is in pieces; he is beside himself with worry.

Komarov is in a similar state. Fear and rage at the level to which his own brother has stooped, burn through his heart, burn through his mind. He will not lose Mac; he will do everything in his power to get her back. He will do everything in his power to teach his monstrous brother a lesson that he will never forget. Nobody messes with his witch; nobody messes with his McKinley.

In the eyes of the public, Sascha is employed by Komarov as a general gofer, but in truth Sascha is so much more. He is a skilled marksman and his fighting and tracking skills are phenomenal. He is a trained hunter, mostly a hunter of men. Sascha was seventeen when he came to Komarov from a specialized military school: a school that very few people know about. Children between the ages of six and eight who have no family and are under state care are selected for this school. It is only after being put through rigorous tests that they are even considered. By the time he was seventeen, Sascha's skills surpassed those of any of the elite forces of the world. Such 'Specialists' are very expensive. They do not even exist as far the ordinary person knows, but they are sought-after and bought by the very wealthiest across the world. Komarov could afford one such as Sascha only because of the favors he was owed by some of the most prominent leaders in the country. They acknowledged the sacrifices that Komarov had made for them at massive personal cost, and repaid him by acquiring for their loyal friend the finest Specialist that the school had to offer.

"So, what do you think, Sasch? What is the plan?" Komarov has summoned his Specialist to his office. Plans are underway. The sooner they can get Mac back, the better.

"I don't think we should involve the whole town; they will just get hurt and complicate things." Sascha cannot stand still. He is pacing around the office like a caged tiger. Needing to be doing something; needing to get to McKinley.

"We must extract her from right under their noses, just like they did here." The fact that they had managed such a thing still burns in Sascha's heart, consuming him with guilt and regret.

"Mmmm. . . how did that happen, anyway? How did they get past you?"

"Diversions." Sascha had been led on a wild goose chase that night when a few of Borya's men had begun to fight and Sascha went to break it up.

"They know who you are?"

"No. All they know is that I am part of your security."

"Good, good." Komarov stands up and joins Sascha in pacing.

"I do want to teach them a big lesson, though … something that will stop them from ever messing with us again."

"I was thinking exactly the same thing, sir."

Sascha is relieved to start on the planning, to start working towards the complicated extraction, to start on the road that will bring their McKinley back to them. They are in that office for hours, and when they emerge they both have the same smug look on their faces, the same spark of battle in their eyes.

Dr. Tatianna – or Dr. Tatts, as most call her – is short and slightly rotund in stature, with cold, calculating eyes that are mag-nified to an owlish size behind spectacles with strong, round, 'milk bottle' lenses. She has a busy mind and hands that cannot stay still. Her analytical mind runs like a machine, without any emotion to cloud her judgment or sully her conclusions. In as much as it is pos-sible for her to be so, she is excited about the arrival of the Witch of Ivanov. She is keen to continue her studies of the paranormal, aiming ultimately to capture the 'witch' gene that can be used for empowering those who have the money to pay. She cannot wait to get to the girl: to analyze her blood, tissue, and anything else that can be extracted; anything that will fit under her microscope. The study of this girl's mind and brain is of particular interest. The idiot who is funding her for the moment, Borya Komarov, is so far resisting her pleas to have full access to the witch. Dr. Tatts is willing to wait a little while; she can do a general study for now. The doctor worked and trained during the Cold War where she learned primarily that humanity just gets in the way of real science, along with the invaluable lesson that there is more than one way to skin a cat.

A commotion in the passageway has the doctor putting her head out of her lab, and she sees that the area is clogged with Borya's men, one of whom has a small person slung over his shoulder. They make their way to the back room that has been prepared for the witch. Eagerly, Dr. Tatts follows. Bustling up behind them, she issues a flow of instructions in her thin reedy voice; instructions which are blatantly ignored by the men preceding her.

Mac is dropped down onto a bed, and her hands are untied.

"Move it, bozo, we need to get out of here. She can untie her own feet."

"What about her gag? The boss said she has to keep it on."

"No! No!" The doctor is adamant. "She needs to eat and drink; she needs to rest. How am I supposed to work with a specimen in this condition?"

The men back out, none of them daring to take their eyes off *Koldun'ya*. She stares back at them with eyes as hard as gemstones, promising vengeance in the worst possible way.

Chapter 10 – Whatever .... (Rolling Eyes)

At first Mac is grateful to the little doctor, who buzzes around her like an oversized bumblebee. Muttering to herself, the doctor helps Mac undo the ropes that bind her feet so tightly.

"These guys are a bunch of cretins," the doctor mutters. "Surely this was not necessary."

Mac looks around, noticing that the room is nothing but a windowless cell. The door, which has been left open for now, is made of thick metal. Through another open doorway opposite, Mac sees a small bathroom. Lining one wall is an assortment of boxes and crates, containing mostly medical supplies, clothing, and non-perishable foodstuffs. This room is obviously used as a storeroom, as well as for keeping kidnapped witch prisoners.

Dr. Tatts puts a pile of dry clothes on the bed, and instructs Mac to go and take a hot shower before changing into the fresh clothing. Mac does not need to be asked twice. She stands under that shower for long minutes. Although at first the water stings her icy skin, she is soon able to increase the heat, reveling in the feeling that her body is almost melting under the hot, drumming water. She emerges warm and fresh, and dresses quickly. On the bedside table there is a big bowl of delicious-smelling stew waiting for her, along with a jug of chilled water. Mac does not waste any time, and once she has quenched her thirst, she tucks into the food. While she eats, Dr. Tatts sits on a chair opposite, asking her a myriad of questions and making notes on her clipboard at regular intervals. The questions are thorough and invasive.

"How come you want to know about my family?" McKinley is beginning to feel suspicious of this beady-eyed woman who is becoming very pushy and is being far too nosey.

"Just to get perspective," comes the curt reply.

In Mac's mind, Dr. Tatts changes from a busy, buzzing bumblebee, into a sly, sidling spider. The doctor obviously has an agenda and McKinley is not willing to be her happy volunteer.

She clams up and refuses to answer anything more. Dr. Tatts pushes hard, then she sits back and watches Mac with hard little eyes.

"No problem, Miss McKinley. I have ways of getting what I need. Sleep well."

Mac is aware that her head is feeling increasingly thick and heavy, her brain is sluggish, and she is battling to keep her eyes open. The last thought she has as she slips into black oblivion is that the food had surely been drugged and she is now helpless in the hands of a monster disguised as an undersized, busy-body woman.

"McKinley!"

She opens her eyes to find Sascha lying next to her. His head is propped up on one hand and he is smiling down at her, golden sunlight reflecting in his silver eyes.

"Sasch? How did you find me?"

She runs her fingers through his hair, smiling back at him. Somehow, they are outside, in the warm sunshine. It looks like a field near her old home.

"How did we get here?" She frowns at him in confusion.

"I don't know what you are talking about." He laughs, then leans down and kisses her full on the mouth, his lips warm against hers. She slides her hands over his shoulders, feeling the muscles flexing under his t-shirt.

"McKinley!" He is looking intently at her now, his eyes dark with worry and fear. "Mac, you need to wake up."

"Sasch?" McKinley watches in horror as Sascha's face starts to disintegrate, disappearing into a cloud of black smoke and fiery ashes.

"Wake up, Mac." His voice is pleading and desperate.

"Sasch! Wait, don't leave me here!" Her heart is in her throat and her breathing comes in despairing gasps.

"Hold her down, you simpleton twit." The voice seems to come from the deep, black waters of a vast ocean. "I need to tighten these straps and get this needle in; she is starting to wake up."

Mac feels hands pushing roughly down on her shoulders and digging into her legs.

"The boss hasn't cleared you for this."

"He won't care once money and power land in his lap."

"He wants the witch alive; he is expecting the payment for her to arrive any day."

"Don't worry, she will be alive. Just how alive cannot be guaranteed, or the likelihood of damage avoided; it is a sacrifice that needs to be made."

Mac is aware of a roaring pain in her head, while tongues of fire rage through her entire body. The sound of screaming rips through her mind. . . terrified, full of unimaginable pain. It dawns on her with a black crash of panic, that she is the one who is screaming. She is the one in the grip of sheer terror; she is the one in the clutches of a pain that is close to driving her mind over the edge, straight into madness.

"Will you shut her up! I do not need people coming in here."

A large, clammy hand clasps over Mac's mouth, and her eyes fly open. She is in a laboratory of some kind. Lying strapped to a narrow hospital bed, she is surrounded by bags hanging from hooks above her, with each containing a different colored fluid running through various tubes, straight into the veins of her arms and legs.

Once again, McKinley hears the calming voice of her Pops. She closes her mind to the pain and confusion, and opens her senses to her immediate surroundings. There is the hum of a computer near her head, the rapid beeping of a heart monitor, the alarm sounding urgently from the machine monitoring her brain activity. Mac shuts out the excruciating pain crushing her brain. The strong smell of medicine burns the back of her throat and stings her nostrils, and she hears the heavy breathing of the doctor and her helper. As Dr. Tatts moves closer, Mac can see that she is not at all focused on the girl strapped on the bed; instead, her eyes are glued to the monitors above Mac's head. The straps holding her arms down are not very tight, she realizes: the doctor has forgotten to check them in her greed and haste. Slowly, *Koldun'ya* McKinley moves her hand toward the monster doctor. She stretches her fingers out, feeling for the arm of Dr. Tatts. Then, as fast as lightning when she touches the cloth of the lab coat, Mac clasps her fingers around the doctor's wrist. Her special ability to draw pain and suffering out of a person can also be used in reverse. McKinley closes her eyes. Focusing on all her pain and anguish, she forces it straight into the vertically-challenged body of Dr. Tatts.

At first the woman freezes in confusion. Then she realizes that her body is on fire, and indescribable pain engulfs her. Her head feels like it is in a vice. Startled, she sees that the witch has her hand clasped tightly around her wrist. Streams of different colors, the same as those that are being pumped into the body of the girl, are running straight from her hand into the arm of the doctor along with untold pain and extreme mental anguish.

"How are you doing that?" Even now, in the grip of total torture, Dr. Tatts is still the mad scientist. The doctor tries to pull away, tries to free herself, but she is already weakened. With each passing second, the witch is becoming stronger, pumping more and more of the toxins and liquids into the body of the doctor. Pumping more and more of the pain straight into the doctor's system.

Dr. Tatts's breath is coming in rasping gasps now.

"....... It is too much....... The pain......" The doctor groans, then her legs buckle from under her and she collapses to the floor. Mac flicks her gaze up to the face of the astounded assistant. He looks from the striped arm of the doctor down at *Koldun'ya* McKinley, whose eyes are fixed on him, shining hard and fierce. With a yelp of fear, he lets go of Mac as if he had been burned by a branding iron, then runs for his life.

The doctor has gone limp. Her body has taken on most of Mac's pain now; she has absorbed most of the concoctions of torture. Mac releases her and she slumps to the floor, barely breathing. Mac works her hands free from the straps and quickly slides the needles out from her body. The relief is almost immediate. She undoes her legs and swings them down onto the floor. At first her legs feel as if the bones and muscles have turned to jelly, but she manages to make it to the door, staggering like a drunk. She looks cautiously out into the corridor. All is quiet.

Looking down at her clothes, Mac realizes that she is in nothing but a hospital gown. She needs to change before she can do anything else. Guessing at the direction of the back room where she was first held, she moves down the long passageway as fast as she is able, her legs gaining strength with every step. She almost misses the small opening: just a narrow doorway leading into a confined passageway. The sound of shouting echoes from somewhere not too far away, followed by the thump of running feet. The lab assistant must have sounded the alarm. Mac slips quietly through the doorway and hurries to the door at the end. It smells dank and musty, as if she is in a room underground . . . a basement, maybe. The door is unlocked and sure enough, she recognizes the room as the one she had been in earlier. Rooting around in the boxes and crates that are piled against the wall, she pulls out gear that must have been bought from army surplus. Excellent. She can disguise herself as one of the dimwits.

She tucks her hair securely under a cap, and drags on the oversized jacket to hide her slight, womanly shape. The boots are slightly too big for her, causing her to move at a clumping walk. She looks like a short, stomping soldier, with the attitude to go with it. Mmmm .... something is missing though. Right! She will need some sort of weapon. Looking frantically in each of the boxes proves futile; of course they would not keep weapons along with their prisoners. Even for these guys, that would be just plain stupid. She needs something that at least makes her look like she is armed. What soldier runs around with no weapon? In a box on a back shelf, McKinley finds a few old tools. She hauls out a single-socket wheel spanner. If she holds it right, it could look like a gun. From a distance. Maybe.

This is not a good time to linger; she has already been here far too long. Mac hurries to leave the room. If she gets trapped here, there will be no chance of escape.

Keeping to the shadows, she waits while a bunch of guards gallop down the main corridor in the direction of the laboratory. As the last guy goes running past, she quietly makes her way out into the passageway and moves off in the opposite direction.

McKinley has no idea about the layout of the place that she is in right now. She can only guess, and hope that she is heading toward freedom. If she is underground, then she needs to go up. Doesn't she? As hard as she tries to think back, she cannot remember being carried down stairs, of any kind. She would have felt it if they had used an elevator. Maybe she is not underground after all?

This place is a maze. Mac has been wandering around for at least an hour now, and still she has not come across any sign of the outside world. It is as if the whole building has been swallowed up into the earth. As she rounds yet another corner, she is assailed by a strong scent, an all-engulfing smell . . . warm, wet, and metallic. She sees somebody sitting up against a wall a short distance away. Ducking her head back, Mac waits, straining her ears for the slightest sound. Everything is as quiet as the grave, apart from the constant humming of the overhead lighting. She cautiously looks back around the corner. The man is still there, as immobile as death, not a flicker of movement.

Mac edges closer, half expecting it to be a trap, half expecting him to leap up at any second, pointing a hidden weapon at her. She notices the awkward angle of his head, the way his body is slumped. As she approaches, the smell of blood hits her in a wave that engulfs all her senses. She stares down at the man with his empty, lifeless eyes. His throat has been sliced open, his life blood pumped from his body with every beat of his heart until there was nothing left to pump, until his heart seized up and his brain shut down. There is a river of congealing blood running along the length of the corridor. As her eyes follow the gruesome trail, she picks out another slumped figure propped up against the same wall. A dark shadow, as still as death. And another… and another…

Something is going on. Something sinister and deadly. Borya's men all sitting slumped up against the walls, all in the same way, with empty eyes staring, wide and unfocused; sitting in cooling pools of blood, their throats sliced wide open. The strange thing is that no alarm has sounded, nobody seems to have noticed the alarming number of bloody bodies that line the passages.

What is going on? She suddenly feels intensely vulnerable. Avoiding numb-nuts is one thing, but trying to hide from a force that kills unseen and unheard, a threat that is part of the same shadows that she is using to hide herself from her own enemies, is quite another. It crosses her mind that the very disguise that has been keeping her safe from discovery, has now become the total opposite. There is a strong possibility that it has made her a target, and her foe is Death.

Chapter 11 – Be Afraid, Be Very Afraid

Borya Komarov is starting to get very nervous. The reports are coming in thick and fast. All of them very confused, all of them bad. He does not know what is happening, but his men seem to have been scattered by panic and fear. These are hardened criminals, chosen because they have nothing left to lose. Human life for them is as meaningless as that of a flea, to be squashed then discarded without a second thought. The first report is about Dr. Tatianna. From the garbled and confused account provided by her assistant, it appears that the doctor had been messing about with those sadistic concoctions of hers and had taken it upon herself to try them on that imbecilic girl. Whether the girl be demon or witch, normally Borya would not have minded if she were tortured to death. Serve her right. But in this case, she belongs to his brother Dimitri. Borya would like nothing better than to taunt his brother with the girl for as long as possible. The plan was to dangle her just out of his reach for extended periods, until his brother is driven mad with frustration. Until he has been drained of every cent and every possession. Borya was planning to string him along, to send bits of that infernal girl to him every now and again, just to keep the tension up. Borya would have enjoyed the game. He would have enjoyed watching the face of the girl change from innocently angelic to hard and haunted, a face without trust, without hope. Dimitri would never have the nerve to come to see Borya in person: he would never have the nerve to confront him; he would never have the nerve for a rescue attempt. He would hide in that forsaken town of his and watch as his witch was sent back to him, one piece at a time.

Now it seems that these delicious plans have gone up in smoke. Nobody can find the girl. Instead, Borya's army of hardened men seems to be dwindling with every passing second. He wonders if this demon witch girl has anything to do with the disappearances of his men. Nothing can be picked up on the CCTV footage. Nothing can be found. Borya designed his house to confuse the most cunning of enemies. His opulent mansion has been built on top of a maze of passages, intended to confuse and confound. It is only a matter of time before the rats are flushed out of the sewers, then the story will unfold and all the pieces will fall into place.

At that moment, a man wheels in the remains of Dr. Tatts on a bed. The body has been covered with a sheet.

"Sorry to disturb you, Mr. Komarov, but you should probably see this."

As the sheet is drawn down, Borya looks on the face of his ex-doctor and he begins to wonder if there are after all completely inexplicable events in this world. He wonders if there is in fact something to all the nonsense that people harp on about. If these mysterious things do exist, then this must be the darkest and blackest of magics.

"What are all these colors?" Borya leans down to look upon the face of Dr. Tatianna. Her glazed eyes stare lifelessly up, wide open and fixed in a disbelieving expression. Her mouth has been frozen in place at an odd angle, is if she was not sure whether to laugh, cry, or scream. Her skin is dark, with bulging veins spidering her body like so many colored rivers on a map.

"These are the solutions that she had pumping into the veins of the witch."

"How did they end up inside the doctor?"

"*Koldun'ya* of Ivanov, she is very powerful." The man stares at Borya with wide, frightened eyes. "It might be best for you to just let her go, or she might kill us all."

"Mr. Komarov, come in!" A voice, crackling and disjointed, calls him urgently over the radio.

"Komarov. Send, over."

"We have men down in the eastern passages, over."

"Repeat."

"All dead, throats cut…"

"Repeat?"

Sweat starts sliding down his temples and dripping off the end of his nose. Impossible! That must be a mistake. How can that be? There is no way anyone can enter his place without detection. There is no way that his invincible band of men can be overpowered.

This day is becoming a total mess. The idiot of a girl has escaped, his doctor has been killed by a means that is way beyond him, and now his men are turning up dead and he has no idea if it is the witch who is killing them or somebody else entirely. It is time to gather the troops (well, what is left of them) and show a united force. The time for careful tactics and ruthless measures has come.

It takes him the better part of an hour to contact and call in his security force. The numbers have noticeably dwindled. The slain men have been brought in from the passages. Enough is enough. War has been declared, and the gloves are off.

Caught up in the crowd, Mac keeps her head down and clumps along behind the rest of the pack. It won't hurt to see what is going on. Above all, she might finally find the exit to these endless passages. But bringing up the rear, she is feeling particularly vulnerable. The hair at the back of her neck is standing on end and she cannot shake the feeling that they are being tailed. A shadow, sinister and dark, made up of blood and death. Every time she swings around, there is nothing but emptiness... an emptiness that seems full of eyes. She turns, dropping back a few strides. As she lowers her eyes and lengthens her stride, an arm shoots out from nowhere and clamps around her throat, as hard and strong as an iron band, and she is dragged into the shadows, held tightly up against a solid chest. Cold steel, razor-sharp, presses against her throat: the blade of a hunting knife. McKinley draws in a shaky breath. Fighting this person will not achieve anything. Either she will die by the blade of this knife, quick and silent, or, if she somehow frees herself from this maniac, she is sure to be captured again and she will certainly die by some unimaginable means, slow and lingering.

"What are you waiting for? Just do it already," she whispers harshly.

"You suck at being a soldier, *Koldun'ya* McKinley." Lips move against her ear, warm and intimate.

"Sasch?" She whips around in surprise, to see laughing silver eyes, dear and familiar. She is still being held against that hot body, but the knife is no longer at her throat. The arm that held her captive like an iron band has become protective, the fingers caressing her cheek. She turns and clutches at his bloody shirt. She can't help it; she dissolves into tears. They stream down her cheeks in rivers. Slipping her arms around his neck, Mac buries her face against his shoulder and Sascha holds her tightly against his chest as she heaves great gulping sobs.

"Shhh... little witch, you need to be brave just a short while longer... we need to escape this place." His heart is breaking for his brave girl. She should never have had to deal with this kind of trauma. With this death and violence; this devastating cruelty. He knows first-hand, the permanent dark stain it leaves on one's heart.

For once, Mac cannot speak, and she just nods her understanding. She takes deep shuddering breaths, steadying herself, clearing her mind. Now is not the time to be a whimpering, gibbering idiot. She has got to be strong. She has got to be McKinley. *Koldun'ya* McKinley, who holds the power of the sleeping giants of the earth, of the earth itself. Her sobs subside and her tears dry upon her cheeks. She lifts her head and looks up into the face that she adores above all others. For the first time, she notices the black grease of camouflage in thick lines across his blood-splattered face. He is wearing a balaclava that has been pulled up now to reveal his face. Sascha is geared for battle and death. His hi-tech stealth camouflage is drenched with blood; he is armed with a variety of knives and blades; he has a sniper rifle and two handguns.

"Sasch," Mac is frowning at him. She is starting to feel more herself, despite their hazardous surroundings. "You are a little overdressed. You know that all you really need is a wand?"

"Batteries are flat, *Koldun'ya*." He flashes a grin at her, then becomes serious.

"Can you handle a gun, Mac?" He glances with a raised eyebrow at her attempt at a gun, the old wheel spanner that so far seems to have fooled most of Borya's men.

"That is not going to help much, unless you are planning to use it to brain your enemy?"

"Don't mock the spanner, Sasch." Mac grins. "I know how to handle guns," she adds.

Of course, she does. Without another word, Sascha hands Mac one of his handguns. Mac holds the gun with confidence and she immediately checks the chamber, then holds out her hand to Sascha for the missing rounds. Mac has been well taught. Sascha is starting to wonder about Mac's father; he was possibly a lot more than just a wilderness guide.

Now to get out of this hellhole. Home is calling, loud and clear.

"I beg your pardon; say that again." Borya stares at the man, his eyes cold and hard.

"Um, it seems that we have a Specialist in the building. Sir." The man shifts his feet nervously. He regrets being the one to share this nugget of information with Borya Komarov, who has been known to shoot his messengers for a lot less.

"Why the would a Specialist be in my building?"

"We think that he may be in the service of your brother."

"Pah!" Borya scoffs. "My brother would never." He rounds on the man, his face bright red and sweating. "What makes you say such things?"

"There is no sign of the person who is killing the men, Mr. Komarov. Their bodies just appear, with their throats open. No sign of struggle. He moves like a ghost, there is no sound. Just death and blood."

"You are being just a tad dramatic. What about the girl?"

"The same. No sign. The men are thinking that the Specialist in question and the witch are one and the same."

"Impossible!" But the seed has been planted. Could that be true? Borya has reached his limit. His fear and anger have far surpassed the tipping point. He cannot stand being so out of control – and he has felt out of control from the second he laid eyes on his brother's witch in that cursed library.

His men have scattered like rabbits. He is sure that it is only a matter of time before he will be left on his own in this monstrosity of a house that he calls home. Borya dismisses the man with orders to have all the remaining men meet him out front. As he turns to gather papers from his desk, he feels his skin burning icy-cold and blazing hot at the same moment. Right on top of the pile of papers is a note that has been written on his brother's stationery. Borya recognizes Dimitri's handwriting.

'NO MORE. LEAVE WHILE YOU CAN.'

Just those words. Nothing more, nothing less.

Chapter 12 – Wolves And A Blizzard. This Is Russia After All

Sascha and Mac move along the walls, staying in the murky shadows. The goal of causing fear and dissension in the ranks has been more than accomplished. But it has also become a handicap. Men who are doing their own thing, who no longer have a leader or a plan, are unpredictable. Now, the going is slow and enemies are surfacing at random intervals, trigger-happy and spooked beyond the ability to reason clearly. Some have ended up shooting one another. All are making for the outside, for freedom and the safety of open spaces.

Mac can see an open doorway up ahead. Although the weather outside looks wild and suffocatingly cold, the open skies beckon like a drug. But Sascha holds her back. They flatten themselves against the wall, blending into the shadows as a group of men go running out, heading for the outside. No sooner have the men put a foot out of the doorway, than they are mown down by a spray of machine gun fire accompanied by much profanity. Borya Komarov, the boss himself, is lying somewhere under cover, waiting for these cowards and traitors who are fleeing instead of fighting.

Sascha puts his mouth against Mac's ear. "We need to find another way."

Mac rolls her eyes at him. Well, obviously, dude.

Shaking his head, his silver-gray eyes gleaming, Sascha nods back toward the way they came. She may know defense moves and how to handle a weapon as well as any soldier, but she certainly does not know how to take orders like a soldier. Come to think of it, *Koldun'ya* McKinley only takes orders when it suits her; otherwise, she will blatantly ignore even her own boss. Looking at her cheeky face peering up at him from under that ridiculous cap, he wonders why it is that at this most inopportune time, in the midst of lurking enemies and devils, he feels the strongest urge to pull her into his arms and kiss her senseless... As he moves back past Mac, her fingers find his and he halts in mid-step as she lifts them to her lips and kisses them. Then she nods, frowning at him to get a move on. She follows closely, her fingers still entwined with his.

Sascha has a highly-developed sense of direction. The passages are designed to appear deceptively complicated, when in fact the well-used routes are rather straightforward and simple for those who are familiar with the layout. He soon discovers the exit that leads into the main house. All is quiet; only the occasional rattle of a machine gun outside the house breaks the heavy silence that has permeated the rooms like a thick blanket. Mac follows Sascha as he leads her through the house, toward a side door. Grabbing the well-padded jackets that are hanging on hooks near the door, they leave unchallenged. It is all suspiciously easy. Perhaps everyone is trying not to get shot by the boss, who seems to have gone stark raving mad.

The weather outside is horrendous. An Arctic wind driving torrential rain and sleet whistles into every nook and cranny, slamming the ice and rain against every barrier. Mac is grateful for her great oversized jacket, and huddles into the thickly-lined fleece. She never wants to feel cold again. Sascha seems to know where he is going and they run doubled over, keeping low and sticking to as much cover as possible. After thirty minutes, Sascha stops at a thick cluster of trees and underbrush. Hurriedly, he moves branches aside to reveal Mr. Dimitri's large all-terrain hunting vehicle. Mac has never felt so happy to see such a sight in her life. She clambers inside as soon as Sascha unlocks her door and slams the door closed, shutting out the roar of the storm and the fierce, cutting cold.

"Phew! Hectic." Mac has her fisted hands retracted up into the large sleeves. "Come on, Sasch, stop wasting time. Put on the heater before I…" The rest of her words are cut off as Sascha pulls her onto his lap by her giant-sized jacket and starts kissing her frozen face.

"You talk too much, *Koldun'ya* McKinley," he whispers, between kisses. "And you are far too bossy."

"What are you doing?" She stares up at him, her eyes large and glowing.

"Warming you up; you look like you need it."

"Oh, is that what you call it?" She smiles at him, then reaches up and pulls his mouth down onto hers.

"Thank you for coming to find me, Sasch."

"I thought I had lost you, Mac. You are everything to me, you are my life. There is no joy in the world without you in it."

"Phew, I am so hot right now." Mac struggles to remove her jacket. . . not easy in such a confined space. "I meant for you to turn on the car heater, Sasch, not my heater."

Free of the cumbersome jacket at last and ditching her oversized, clumpy boots, Mac climbs back onto Sascha's lap, facing him with her legs either side of his seat. She puts her arms around his neck and pulls him down, kissing him with all the love and adoration that is pouring from her heart. Once again, she cannot seem to get close enough; once again she feels an uncontrollable urge for him to become a part of her.

The idea of living a life without this indomitable madam in it is unthinkable. He gathers her up into his arms and holds her as close as he is able. He cannot stop kissing her. He is well aware that they need to get out of there, put in as much mileage as possible, get out from the clutches of this madman. But right now, this is exactly where he wants to be. . . with McKinley warm and soft in his arms, kissing him back, giving her all, in typical McKinley fashion.

"Mac." Sascha leans back. He sifts his fingers though her hair and trails a finger down her smooth cheek. "Let's go home."

Smiling, she hugs him, holding him close and kissing him on the side of his neck. Then she moves over to her side of the vehicle and straps in for a wild ride. The vehicle growls to life and Sascha backs it out of the wooded cover. Immediately they are assailed by the full might of a Siberian storm. Visibility: Zero.

The vehicle is of course fitted with all the latest in off-road technology, so even though nothing can be seen through the blizzard, Sascha drives with confidence. The going is slow; there is nobody following, no sign of life within the immediate surroundings. But Sascha does not trust Borya Komarov for one second and he expects the man to retaliate, one way or another. Right now, their escape is shielded by the raging storm, but it will be just a matter of time before Borya comes at them with more fury than any Siberian storm can offer. Mac has cooled down substantially; she turns up the heat and huddles under her very large jacket. They are silent for the first slow miles, occupied with their own thoughts. The full wrath of a storm on the Siberian tundra is fearsome and the hazards are many, but at last there are signs that the weather is easing. Sascha glances at Mac; she seems unusually quiet and withdrawn.

"You okay?" He leans across and tucks a wayward strand of dark hair behind her ear. She turns to him, her face serious. There is none of the usual spark, none of the usual fire.

"I killed her, Sasch." McKinley's eyes fill with tears that spill over, sliding down her cheeks. She heaves a shuddering sigh. Now that things are quiet and she has time for thought, the hopelessness, the fear, the blood, and violence that have surrounded her in the past days crash down onto her mind all at once.

"What are you talking about, Mac?"

"I killed Dr. Tatts. I did not have to take it so far; I could have stopped as soon as she passed out." Mac's eyes are almost black with the magnitude of emotion weighing heavily on her conscience, so dark that they are almost the same color. "I kept hold of her, Sasch, until she was beyond help. I kept hold of her until I was sure she could not come back."

Sascha glances across at her. He has no idea what she is speaking about, only that she is feeling deep sorrow. Mac is always so strong, so positive. One forgets that she is just a young person who has never had to deal with the evil and cruelty of this world. She has never before had to face the blatant murderousness and ruthless bloodlust of men like these. The extreme trauma of the events of these past hours is weighing heavily on her mind, heavily on her heart.

Mac looks up. "Sasch!" she shouts, and braces herself against the dashboard. Sascha's reactions are lightning-fast. He knows that he cannot brake, and swerving is out of the question. The dark shapes of wolves are just visible crossing the road in front of them, and the animals stop and stare into the headlights of the approaching vehicle. Frozen in fright and blinded by the sudden brightness. The wheels slide onto a sheet of black ice spanning the road and the vehicle starts to spin, picking up momentum as it goes. The instruments buzz loudly in alarm.

"Hang on, Mac!" Sascha shouts. He knows this road; he knows that to leave it will be very bad, very bad indeed. He fights to regain control but there is not much that can be done once you are sliding on an icy road. The vehicle careens off the road, its wheels catching on the rocks under the snow, flipping it over. The momentum makes it roll twice more. The noise is deafening... the smashing glass, the roar of the engine, the screech of metal as the car ploughs over hidden boulders and slams into a rocky outcrop. The silence that follows is as loud as a bomb blast.

Chapter 13 – Letting The Cat Out Of The Bag

*M*ac is woken by an urgent whispering in her ear, the voice panicked and pleading. It is the voice of Tetya Anya.

"Please, my lady, you need to help." Anya's face is wet with tears, her hands shaking.

"Please, you must come. I am afraid he may not live much longer." Her desperate voice is loud now in Mac's ear.

Mac slowly climbs out of her bed, her bare feet cold on the floor, and follows Anya out onto a snow-covered road. The shadows of wolves slinking in the darkness just beyond the reach of headlight beams. An all-terrain vehicle parked haphazardly in the drifting snow. Mac cannot help but notice the large amount of blood splattered inside the vehicle, the congealed pools of blood around the driver's seat. Anya opens the door and pulls Mac inside. Everything is dark and icy; she can just make out the shape of a man draped over the steering wheel.

"Anya, why have you left him alone in the dark? It is so cold in here."

"I know, my lady. I thought it best to fetch you; only you can help"

The snow around the man is already soaked with blood. He is unconscious, his breathing shallow and rapid. When Mac peels the sodden heavy jacket aside, she sees that his clothes are just bloody shreds, clinging to his lacerated flesh.

"It was a bear?" She starts removing what remains of his clothing.

Anya takes Mac's hands in hers. "Do not give up; stay strong and fight with him."

McKinley's eyes fly open. She is still strapped into her seat. Cold air and snow flurries are coming in through the smashed windscreen, covering her with a thin layer of white. The engine has stalled, but the headlights still shine into the misty darkness. It feels as if it was hours ago that the world went spinning out of control, hours since she and Sascha were in one another's arms. A steady sound of dripping seeps into her confused thoughts, then a low mournful howl of a wolf echoes through the night. Turning her head, Mac can just make out the dim form of Sascha. He is leaning on the steering wheel, his face turned toward her. A face that is covered in blood.

"Sasch!" Mac struggles to free herself from her seatbelt. The latch is jammed and she loosens it from the top and slips through. Scooting over to Sascha, she checks his vitals. His breathing is shallow and he is unconscious. The vehicle had slammed up against a pile of rocks, smashing Sascha's door and buckling on impact, shattering the window and covering him with broken glass. Mac needs to check him over; she needs to see where all the blood is coming from. She checks everything that she can without moving him. Finding that the blood is seeping from superficial wounds and there is nothing life-threatening, she carefully pushes him back into the seat, taking care to support his neck and head.

"Sascha!" Mac calls him again. "Stay with me, Sasch."

She opens his snow-sodden jacket and moves his shirt aside. There is an ominous bubbling sound to every shallow breath he takes. A strong feeling of déjà vu floods her. Anya, it was Anya who had woken her up. It was Anya who came to her in a waking nightmare. Mac understands. Sascha's fine body is not covered with the deep lacerations of bear claws, but his flesh is bruised and distended in places. Sascha's body is as broken and bloodied as it was in her dream; not on the surface, but under his skin and flesh. He has internal injuries that are fast draining him of life.

Mac finds the lever and manages to push Sascha's seat as far back as it will go. There are blankets on the back seat. She removes his soaking clothes, and taking her own big, padded jacket off, she shifts up close to his shivering body. There is hardly any space, but she manages to fit her body in alongside his. She tucks the blankets around them, trying to trap as much heat as possible. Lastly, she drapes her thick, padded jacket over the top, then puts her arms around Sascha, trying to connect as much bare flesh as she can. She places her hands flat on Sascha's back, directly over his heart, and closing her eyes, she breathes deeply. She pictures in her mind the pain in his body running black and thick, contaminating the purity of his blood. She concentrates on drawing the pain out, taking it into her own body. She can fight it; she is strong and powerful. She can defeat it. She pictures all the ruptures knitting together, she pictures the blood draining back into his system, she pictures his crushed ribs knitting together, she pictures his lungs free of blood, inflating. Mac pictures every part, mending and healing.

Sascha's eyes flick open. He is feeling warm and pain-free. He cannot understand it; the last thing he remembers before he passed out, was being in excruciating and unbearable pain. He hears soft whimpering sounds close to his ear and turning his head, he looks on the face of McKinley. She is lying next to him, her eyes tightly shut. As Sascha watches, she becomes feverish and hot. Sweat drips down her face; her fine hair clings in wet tendrils to her neck. Heat and redness appear on her skin. As his pain subsides, so Mac seems to be suffering more and more. Her skin comes up in red and angry welts as she tightens her arms around his shoulders and presses her hands more firmly onto his back. Now she is no longer hot, but is shivering within the cocoon of blankets that she has tucked around the two of them.

It seems impossible to Sascha at first; it seems far-fetched and crazy. Is she absorbing the pain from his body? Is she taking his pain upon herself? Is she absorbing his cold, and transferring her heat to him? Even though her eyes are tightly closed, tears squeeze out from under her long, dark lashes and drip down her pale, frozen cheeks.

"No, no, Mac!" Sascha cannot believe it. She is giving her life to him; she is dying before his very eyes. "Mac! Don't do this!" He is panicking now. He recalls the day that they helped Lenna, Anya mumbling something about the girl being far more than she seems; he recalls what Mac was telling him about the doctor. She had given too much then; is she taking too much now?

Sascha tries to pull away from her, tries to break the contact, but Mac will have none of it.

"No, Sasch, not yet. I am not done with you yet." She pulls him closer.

"Mac, open your eyes, my little witch."

"You still have pain..."

"No, you are feeling the pain that I am feeling for you. The pain I feel having to watch you suffering to save me." He kisses her cold lips. "Let go, my beautiful girl, you can rest now."

Her eyes fly open, shining deep and rich. "I thought I was going to lose you." Her voice is barely audible, hoarse and weak.

"Thank you, McKinley." He pulls her close to him, tucking the blankets around them. He starts kissing her face. "Mac..."

"Mmm..." She is exhausted. Though they are stranded in a wrecked vehicle in the middle of a frozen desert, with wolves circling around them and a madman somewhere behind them, she feels completely safe in the arms of Sascha. Sighing, she puts her face against his neck and breathes in the warmth of everything that makes her world turn, that makes her heart beat, that makes her soul sing. A deep slumber overtakes her, and she gladly releases her hold on reality and sinks down into the comforting blackness.

Chapter 14 – Cookies and Goggles

It is hours before Mac surfaces, but it is still dark outside. She is disoriented. She remembers passing out on the front seat of the wrecked vehicle, with Sascha's arms holding her close. Now, she finds herself wrapped in blankets lying in the back of the car where all the windows are intact and the doors secure. She is being held by strong arms, a warm, hard body against her back. Sascha must have put her here. Turning her head, she looks straight into the silver sheen of his eyes.

"You are awake." He smiles. "The wolves were getting far too brave; besides that, it was getting a little frosty up front."

"Good idea, Sasch." She smiles back. "What time is it?"

"Just before dawn. I will see if I can get this poor old wreck started as soon as it gets a little lighter, and hopefully we can get it home."

"It will start!" Mac laughs. "If I can get that old rust-bucket tractor of Farmer Novikov going, I am sure we can get this going."

Sascha looks down at this crazy, beautiful lunatic of a girl. He has always wondered how she got that tractor going, but he won't ask: it is bound to be a very long and complicated story.

Neither of them feels the need to sleep, and they lie together chatting and laughing until the weak, watery sun starts making a tentative appearance. The weather has lifted for now, and it is just light enough to see. Rummaging through a bag of emergency supplies, Mac comes up with some dry clothing – enough to help keep the cold out anyway. The two clamber out of the car and get to work. Home is calling; they are just hours away.

Anya is busy in the kitchen. She likes to bake when she is worried, and right now all available surfaces are piled high with every kind of biscuit and cookie that one can think of. There is a sound at the door and Mr. Komarov puts his head through the doorway. Before he can open his mouth, Anya rushes toward him, wiping her floury hands on her apron. Her red, swollen eyes plead with the boss to have good news for a change and a million questions come tumbling out of her mouth. As soon as he can get a word in edgeways, Komarov takes his housekeeper's hand and again tells her that there is no news, that the tracker on the vehicle seems to have malfunctioned, so he has no idea where they can be.

"Oh no, no, sir, I do not know anything about trackers and stuff, but surely we can drive to where the last lot of co-ordinates was reported. We need to do something."

"Funny enough, that is my idea as well. Grab your coat, Anya, dress warmly. We are going to go and find our witch and her soldier."

Komarov pulls up near the kitchen door, driving an all-terrain vehicle. He has three such vehicles, all state-of-the-art, fitted with all the gadgets. He is very sure that Mac took one of them on a joy-ride through town a few months after she first arrived. The evidence is a blurred photo from an old speed camera that had been set up years ago and then forgotten about. A man who works for the traffic department brought him the photo, looking to slap him with a speeding ticket. Luckily it was very bad quality, so the proof was inconclusive. But it sure looked like his vehicle and that smiling face peering over the dashboard, obscured by the grainy shadows, looked extremely familiar.

Anya has a tower of boxes and packets with her. At his questioning look, she proudly states that she thought to bring some food for the road .... mostly just biscuits and cookies, she admits.

The wreck is causing much frustration. It starts but then keeps spluttering to a shuddering silence until, after many attempts, *Koldun'ya* McKinley marches straight up to the front of the wreck and gives the tire a hefty kick.

"If you don't start now, you heap of scrap, we will leave you for the wolves. I am sure they would love to make a den out of you." She stomps around the car, and gives the opposite tire a vicious kick. "And mark my words, those wolves will rip up your very fine leather seats, and shred your fancy tires."

With that, the vehicle immediately starts up then purrs like a kitten. Sascha laughs his head off.

It takes a lot of maneuvering to get the wreck out of the snow drifts and over the treacherous terrain, but after more false starts than anyone is prepared to count, the vehicle eventually makes it out onto the road. There is much shouting and whooping inside the car, the wild celebration echoing across the snowy wasteland. Mac gives Sascha a big, juicy kiss on the lips, then frowns at him.

"Come on, Sasch, I want to go home. What are you waiting for?"

Grinning from ear to ear, Sascha puts the wreck into gear and they head for home.

They cannot go too fast, considering the state of the vehicle. There is no windscreen, which makes the going tricky. Especially when it starts raining a couple of hours into the trip. Mac again digs in the supplies at the back and produces two pairs of goggles.

"What are these doing in this box , Sasch?" Who on earth would possibly think to put safety goggles into a hunting vehicle?

"Oh." He turns to her, his face serious. "Those goggles are in case our witch gets captured by the evil brother and during her rescue, the windscreen gets smashed, and we have to drive our get-away car without one."

Mac stares at him, her eyes narrowed, then shrugs a shoulder.

"Fine. But I see you forgot the witch's broom. That is a very important item when rescuing witches, Sasch."

She hands him a pair of goggles, snaps hers on, then turns to him, her eyes looking ghoulishly at him through the large plastic lenses.

"This is much better. Good thinking." She stares out at the road for five minutes then turns to him again. "It would have been better if you had got ones with their own little wipers, though."

After a while McKinley doesn't know if the goggles really are such a grand idea. They keep steaming up. She and Sascha are starving, and dying for a hot cup of coffee. She tries to remember the last time she ate – it was that evil, drugged stew from Dr. Tatts. Seems like years ago.

Sascha is battling. His body, although it has been miraculously healed, has been through extensive trauma. He would be a frozen corpse by now if it were not for his darling Mac. Then he was awake most of the night, keeping the wolves at bay, watching out for Borya and his minions. Guarding his McKinley as she slept, exhausted and drained to her limits, both emotionally and physically.

Just when Sascha is thinking that he cannot go one mile farther, they notice a speck in the distance. A vehicle is approaching at speed. There is nowhere to hide, nowhere to run. The road is straight, running over a flat wasteland of endless snow. They can only hope that those approaching are on their own mission and not interested in the wreck that is hobbling along the road, trying not to fall apart.

Sascha pulls over and checks his weapons. They do not want to be left stranded on this desolate road, miles from anywhere. Mac still has her handgun, and she does the same. They sit in silence and wait. The approaching vehicle looms closer, showing no sign of slowing. As it roars past, a mad woman hangs halfway out the window, the wind whipping her graying hair, yelling at the top of her voice there is a brief glimpse of huge laughing grin.

"Was that *Tetya* Anya?" Mac laughs, hardly daring to believe her eyes.

The vehicle that flashed past them screeches to a halt amid a cloud of flying snow, then it backs up. The occupants of both vehicles just stare at one another, huge smiles on their beaming, happy faces.

"Anyone want a cookie?" Anya is the first one to speak.

Chapter 15 – Home

Ivanov – Eastern Russia (Some Weeks Later).

The usual morning meeting is underway.

"I have had word about my brother, Borya." Dimitri Komarov leans back in his chair and flicks his pen around in his fingers. The three standing in his office shift uncomfortably and wait for further information.

"He has fled the country; he will not be back. I do not know where he has ended up; I do not want to know – I do not care."

There is a general sigh of relief. Then Komarov turns to his witch.

"McKinley!"

She is standing between Anya and Sascha as usual, with that ever-present grin on her face.

"I hear that the 'Foothills' have finally arrived. Does that mean anything to you?"

For a change, Mac is struck dumb. Her grin has frozen on her face and that cheeky glint in her eyes has now changed to a gleam of pure surprise and happiness. Anya and Sascha are staring down at their shoes, trying to keep from laughing, trying to hide the fact that they are all in on the surprise.

"The Foothills?" Mac is not sure that she heard Mr. Dimitri clearly.

"I believe that they are in the library as we speak."

Koldun'ya McKinley stares at Mr. Dimitri for a few seconds more, a huge smile lighting her face. Then she starts to laugh. With a whoop of joy, she skips around the huge desk, and gives the very surprised Komarov a tight hug.

"Thank you, Mr. Dimitri," she whispers.

"Mr. Komarov," he automatically corrects her, as he pats her awkwardly on the back.

She releases him, then grabs Sascha and Anya in an all-encompassing hug on her way out of the office. She gallops full speed down the stairs. They can hear her whooping and yelling all the way down.

"Well." Komarov looks at the other two, who are grinning widely at him. "I guess that concludes the meeting for this morning. You can get out now."

When Mac bursts into the library she is accosted by five hurricanes.

"I can't believe you are all here!"

Everyone is speaking at once, the house echoes with shouts of laughter, and the warmth of family seeps into every corner.

"Mac!"

"Mom! How did you guys get here? I was not expecting to see you for months."

"Well, Mr. Komarov has been very kind. He sent Sascha to fetch us."

"Sasch? Why, that conniving sneak!" Mac laughs.

The party is in full swing. The main street has been transformed into a massive banqueting area, complete with tables laden with platters of food. There is a live band on a raised platform and a dance floor big enough to contain most of the town. Their most treasured possession has been returned to them unharmed, along with fantastic stories of her awesome power. The stuff that legends are made of. Already the games that the kids are playing are no longer the usual cops and robbers, but now feature *Koldun'ya* and her Bodyguard against the Useless Army. Nobody wants to belong to the Useless Army of course, and a lot of discussion and negotiation takes place before any game can begin. The younger of the Foothills have joined forces with Lenna's kids; as thick as thieves, the boys are the terrors of the town.

Koldun'ya McKinley and her bodyguard Sascha are at last married; the danger and life-threatening experiences they shared mean the two could not face another second apart from one another. The double celebration will be one that is not easily forgotten.

Dimitri Komarov is sitting at the top table surrounded by family warmth that he never dreamed he could ever be a part of again . . . the loving smiles and bursts of laughter, the shining and happy faces, the easy touching of hands onto arms, the spontaneous hugging and a lot of good natured teasing. Mac's mother and all her many siblings are moving to Ivanov to live. Komarov finds himself looking forward to many joyful Sunday lunches and special occasions along with everything else that accompanies a large and happy family.

Anya too is finding it almost impossible to contain her joy. It is a well-known secret that her cooking has the amazing effect of allowing two hearts to find one another, of welding them together with an unbreakable bond. She leans back and smiles with satisfaction. Her cooking never fails. Mmmm.......her gaze falls on her boss and Mac's Mom........perhaps her work is not over yet......

McKinley

McKinley, the witch of Ivanov, is at this very moment sitting in Sascha's lap. Their arms hold one another tightly, their smiles are only for each other, their eyes are shining with complete love and devotion. A very far cry from the tough, super-killer Specialist and the most wicked witch in the whole of Russia, if not, then the whole, entire world!

Chapter 16 – Conclusion

Dear Miss McKinley Orlov

*T*hank you for your submission for our Romantic Series. Unfortu-
nately, your submission cannot be published by us. (Or anyone.)
Your romantic descriptions are way over the top, and there is no way
that any of this is credible. Also, illustrations were not needed, especially those that don't make a bit of sense. And no, we are not liable for
burnt-out computers.

*You might want to try the Erotica Genre; I am sure they will find
you most entertaining.*

Wishing you all the best of luck (You will need it).

Kindest Regards

Ethel Jemima

EDITOR, Romance Inc.

Dear Ethel Jemima

Thank you for your mail. I appreciate the very constructive criticism. Just one word of advice from the bottom of my heart: if you ever kissed Sascha, if you were ever that lucky, then everything I have sent to you will make a lot of sense. Including the photo of the burnt-out laptop.

Wishing you all the best of luck as well

Kindest regards

Mrs. McKinley Orlov-Volkova

P.S. Sascha was my test subject and consultant on the matter. I highly recommend that you get yourself one too.

P.P.S. Sorry, Sascha is unavailable.

THE END

AKNOWLEDGMENTS

Thank you to my wonderful friend Fiona Rom for her skillful editing.

Thank you, Evan and the Publication Consultants team for all their hard work and great advise.

Thank you Ron for all you do to keep everything under control.